# Midwife in Behruz

## by

## Judy Meadows

**Midwife in Behruz**

Cover Art by *Diana Carlile*

The Wild Rose Press, Inc.
PO Box 708
Adams Basin, NY 14410-0708
Visit us at www.thewildrosepress.com

Publishing History
First Champagne Rose Edition, 2017
Print ISBN 978-1-5092-1740-3
Digital ISBN 978-1-5092-1741-0

Published in the United States of America

### And do you use words like that

when you talk to your American fiancé?"

"Hmmm. No." She fussed with loose tendrils of hair again, and then, apparently giving up on the ponytail, she pulled off the band that held it and let her hair fall free around her shoulders. "I don't suppose I do. He uses a wide assortment of words to refer to the male reproductive organ himself, but I think he'd be a bit uncomfortable if I started talking about *penises*."

"I'm glad to hear that. It makes me feel less backward."

"Backward?"

He straightened a stack of papers on his desk. "I'm aware that people in your culture are more open than we are about matters related to sexuality. People of my culture must seem quite inhibited to you."

She settled her hair behind her shoulders. Glints of auburn shone from the thick waves. "No, not to me. I don't think *inhibited* is the word I would use. I'd say people of your culture are more *respectful* of sexuality. I imagine more of the mystery and sensuality of sex has been retained."

*Mystery and sensuality.* That brought rather disturbing images to his mind. He saw a seduction scene as she might imagine it, a scene in which his culture was exotic and mysterious. And *sensual*—with incense and brooding music and silken robes—maybe in the desert in a sheik's tent, with rugs and cushions and clusters of grapes.

A dreamy fever clouded her eyes and a fresh bloom crept across her cheeks. Was she imagining that same scene? Was he in it?

## Dedications

To my dear friend
who advised me on cultural details,
Bee Sadeghian.

~\*~

And to my husband Jim,
who understands…

## Acknowledgments

The text uses quotes from the Persian poet Rumi (who died in 1273) with permission from the translator of his work, Coleman Barks.

Thanks to Coleman Barks for permission to quote his translations of the Persian poet Rumi.

Prologue

A wedding. A *royal* wedding.

Layla clutched the invitation to her heart. *I'm going to Behruz. Finally.*

She'd seen the gold-embossed card on the mantel when she let herself into her mother's house. Now Mary came to greet her. "Hello, darling. I see you found the invitation."

"Yes, and I'm going."

"I'm not surprised." Mary led Layla to the kitchen and filled a teakettle with water. "You've always wanted to return to Behruz. This is a perfect excuse."

Layla selected two cups from the cabinet. "The timing is perfect. The wedding is a week after my last day of work."

"I don't think anyone else in the family will go. Olivia can't travel during her last trimester, Suzi is too busy, Salma can't leave when school is just starting, and I'll be involved in the benefit gala for the San Francisco Public Library. I've already been to two of Abu-Khan's weddings anyway. I went to the second one when he married that Iranian film star and the third when he married Olivia's sister."

"Were there lots of parties and lavish dinners?"

Mary's gaze drifted away. "There were lavish dinners, but I'm afraid they were formal and rather boring."

1

Layla chuckled. "Well, they won't be boring for me. I don't care if no one else in the family goes. It's my turn. I haven't been back since Daddy died." It had been over twenty years. Layla was a happy, successful, totally *American* woman, yet she felt she'd left a piece of her heart in that faraway land. She yearned to see the country of her roots, to experience *who she was* in that country.

They sat at the kitchen table with their tea. Mary said, "You were only seven when we left. Do you remember Behruz at all?"

"Not much. I remember the garbage man. When we heard his cry, we kids would run down to the street with the garbage and watch while he dumped it into a bag on the back of his camel. I remember the palace, but I hardly remember Abu-Khan at all. He seemed kind of scary to me." A vague image of her father came to her mind: a tall presence holding her hand, guiding her along busy sidewalks. "I remember going with Daddy to buy bread."

"Are you sure you have time for a trip? You'll be awfully busy in September—getting ready for your wedding, moving to Dallas and looking for a new job."

"I'll just get to Dallas a few weeks later, that's all."

"Will Dan be okay with that?"

"Yes." Of course. Dan would be happy for her. This would be her first real vacation in years. And she'd be going to Behruz. For a royal wedding. "Maybe I'll spend a month there."

"You'll be bored silly," Mary said. "What do you think you'll do in Behruz City for a whole month?"

"I don't know. I don't care if all I do is sit in the park." The trip would be a pilgrimage. It would complete her in some way. She had to do this before she married Dan.

Chapter One

Mom had been right about the boring dinners. Would this one never end? The ambassador from Iran was giving a speech, praising Abu-Khan and his regime and asking Allah to rain blessings on the betrothed couple. His speech wasn't much different from the four that preceded it. How many more would there be?

Fortunately there was a break after the Iranian ambassador's speech while tea and melon were served. A buxom middle-aged woman sitting across from Layla asked, "So, my dear, how do you know the bride?"

"Oh, I don't know the bride. That is, I just met her last night." It was a natural assumption, really—that she was a friend of the bride. She and Mina were the only two people under the age of fifty at the table. "Actually, I'm related to the groom."

Everyone within earshot turned to look at her. Layla was wearing her dressiest outfit, a scoop-necked silk top and velvet skirt, but still, surrounded by women wearing designer gowns, she felt underdressed. A man in a military uniform leaned so far toward her he knocked over the woman's water glass.

"Oh." The woman made an ineffectual swipe at the spilled water with her napkin. "I thought you were American."

Layla reached across the table with her own napkin to help with the spill. "It's complicated. You're right, I

4

am American, at least mostly. My mother is American, but my father was Behruzi. He was Abu-Khan's half-brother." She quickly added, "They had the same mother." It was an important distinction. The people at the table would have found her far more interesting if her father and Abu-Khan shared a father, because that would mean she had royal blood in her veins. As it was, she was a commoner.

Before anyone could ask another question, their attention was drawn to the head of the table where one of Abu-Khan's generals was about to speak.

They were in the largest dining room in the palace at a table that sat about sixty. The brightness of the room affected Layla like an overdose of caffeine. Everything glittered: the huge chandeliers that hung heavily above them, the fine glassware, the polished silver, the elegant jewelry worn by the women, even the brass buttons on the servants' uniforms. And gold-framed mirrors on the walls reflected all that splendor. The conversation and laughter were as bright as the chandeliers and mirrors. She felt a little dizzy.

Dizzy and tired. It was her third day in Behruz and already her second formal dinner. She hadn't yet recovered from the long trip.

After the final speech was delivered, Layla lined up with everyone else to greet the happy couple.

"Hello, my dear," Abu-Khan said when it was her turn to pay her respects. He was beaming. Was this the dour, arrogant sultan she'd been hearing about all her life?

Following the lead of the other women, she bowed her head and curtsied. Then she prepared to greet the bride-to-be, but Abu-Khan took her hand in his two

5

large paws and leaned toward her. It almost seemed he was going to kiss her on the cheek, but instead he whispered in her ear, "Come to my office tomorrow morning at ten. There's something I want to discuss with you."

"All right." What was that about? Abu-Khan turned his attention to the next guest in line, so Layla congratulated his fiancé and complimented her beautiful gown.

During their brief conversation at dinner the previous night, Layla found she liked Mina. The bride-to-be appeared to be a few years younger than Layla, probably in her early twenties, but she wasn't as naïve and innocent as Layla had expected.

Abu-Khan must be in his fifties, so the age difference was shocking, or at least it would be back home. It was probably more acceptable here in Behruz. No one at the dinner showed any concern. Abu-Khan seemed quite besotted with Mina—that might give the young bride a little power in the relationship—and Mina appeared to be a bit smitten herself. Maybe she wasn't marrying him *just* for his wealth and power.

When Layla finished with the reception line, she sprinted up the wide, carpeted steps of the grand staircase to her room on the third floor. She wondered what Abu-Khan wanted to see her about, but there would be no answer to that question until tomorrow. She calculated the time difference and saw she could call Dan—he'd be just waking—but she was exhausted, and the bed beckoned...

Dan won.

"I'm so tired I can hardly talk, but I just wanted to hear your voice," she said.

"I miss you, kiddo. You should be here with me. I don't know why I let you make this crazy trip."

What could she say? He was right; it was crazy. Yet nothing could have stopped her.

Dan continued, "It's great to hear from you, but I can't really talk now. I was just leaving for work. Hurry up and get your butt to Dallas, darlin'."

Darlin'? Was he developing a Texas accent after only five months in Texas?

When she went downstairs the next morning, Abu-Khan's personal assistant, an industrious young man named Omid, scanned her casual attire—jeans and a T-shirt—with a slight lip-curl of disapproval. Should she have dressed formally? She'd thought of the planned meeting as a chat with her uncle, not as an audience with the sultan, but now she wondered if she got it wrong. "Good morning, *khanoum*," Omid said. "You'll have to wait a while. The sultan is in conference with his advisors." Omid made the feminine title *khanoum*, which was normally used to show respect, sound slightly insolent. He gave her a bright, false smile that revealed a set of glaringly white teeth.

"Can I sit while I wait?" she asked.

"Yes of course, khanoum." Omid indicated a little waiting room across the corridor, a room filled with thick carpets, ornate mirrors, and brocaded tapestries. She sat in an antique chair upholstered in velvet, facing the open doorway so she could see when the advisors left.

"Omid?" she interrupted him as he prepared to leave. "Could you tell me what happened to Nur?" All her life she'd heard about Nur, the man who'd served as Abu-Khan's assistant for as long as anyone in her family could remember.

"He retired a year ago, khanoum, and he died last spring."

"Oh." She would have to tell her mother.

After Omid left, she pulled her Kindle from her pocket and started to read. Half an hour later, three men in military uniforms with medals and ribbons plastered across their chests came from Abu-Khan's office. They backed out, bowing and muttering obsequious remarks: "Thank you, Excellency" and "May Allah rain blessings upon you, Exalted One."

Crap. She should have dressed more formally. Omid returned to tell her she could see the sultan now. He led her into Abu-Khan's office, where he bowed and announced, "Khanoum Shirvani to see you, Excellency."

She bobbed down in a repeat of the curtsy she'd used at the dinners. Abu-Khan scanned her appearance with a look of disdain similar to Omid's.

He motioned for her to sit in the elaborately carved chair across the desk from him. A portrait of his father, the "old sultan," scowled from the wall behind. There was a strong resemblance between the two men. They had the same thickening at the waistline, the same prominent beak of a nose, the same piercing eyes, the same arrogant chin-raised tilt of the head, and the same thick hair—though the old sultan's hair was almost white, while Abu-Khan's was dark except for a little gray at the temples.

Abu-Khan made stiff small talk for a few minutes. Was she recovered from her long journey? Was she enjoying her stay? Was the room to her liking? Was she comfortable? He told her the wing where her room was located had been destroyed during the rebellion a few years ago and had been rebuilt when peace was restored.

She answered all his questions with monosyllables. Where on earth was this conversation leading?

Abu-Khan drummed his fingers on the desk and leaned back in his chair. He swiped his fingers through his hair, leaving furrows in the lacquered mass. "I guess you're wondering why I've asked you to meet with me." His hand raked through his hair again. How could this powerful man be nervous about talking to *her*?

"Yes." Layla certainly was wondering.

"I understand you're a doctor," Abu-Khan said.

"No, not exactly. I'm a midwife. I deal with health issues related to childbirth, and I deliver babies in the hospital like a doctor, but—"

Abu-Khan gave an impatient little throat-clearing cough. "So you know all about *female matters*?"

"Yes, I guess you could say that."

Color rose to his face. The great, arrogant sultan was blushing. "So then, you know about how babies are made? I mean…about the medical aspects?"

Layla stifled a grin. "Yes, I believe I have a pretty good understanding of the process."

"Okay. Good." His fingers were in his hair again, mangling it further, then trying to pat it back into place. "I guess I have some questions about this matter of *getting* a woman pregnant." His color deepened. After working as a midwife and teaching childbirth classes for six years, Layla was comfortable talking about this subject and she knew how to make other people comfortable with it too. "I think I can answer any questions you might have," she said in her reassuring,

9

professional voice.

"As you may know, my first two wives had difficulty conceiving."

"Did they conceive?"

He picked up a pen and drew a lopsided star on his desk pad before muttering, "Actually no."

"Okay. And your third wife, Karen?"

"Well, there was the one child, Jamal, the one who died, but..."

She spoke in her kind, midwife voice. "I know about Jamal, Abu-Khan. I know he was adopted, and I know he's still alive."

He lurched back in his chair. "You know?"

"Yes, Olivia told me."

"She had no right," he cried, the arrogant sultan again. The lead of his pencil snapped, and they both looked down. There was a gouge in the paper.

"I presume she told my mother, but I don't think she told anyone else. She didn't mention it to me until I was planning this trip. She wouldn't let me come here without knowing, well...everything."

"Oh, I see." His brow furrowed in concentration. He was no doubt imagining what *everything* might entail.

"So three wives have failed to conceive." She used her professional voice again, making the conversation less personal. "And you're hoping to have better luck with Mina?"

"Yes. Is there a medicine that would make the whole, um, *baby-making* system work better?"

"There might be some ways that medical science could help. I think we should start by getting a sample to see if the basic ingredients for baby making are present."

Abu-Khan attacked his hair again. "A sample? Of what?"

"Semen. It's the stuff that's ejaculated by the male during sex. Do you know how that works to impregnate the woman?"

Abu-Khan straightened up and made a harrumphing sound in his throat. "Yes, of course."

The distress on his face suggested he might actually have some questions. "Maybe I should review the process, just to be sure we're on the same page."

"Okay, go ahead if you want to."

Layla explained what happens when semen enters a woman's body, staying in teacher mode and making little sketches on his desk pad to illustrate. Abu-Khan squirmed in his chair, tortured his hair, and fidgeted with his pencil, but he listened intently and bent over her sketches with apparent fascination.

When she was done, he said, "Okay. I can give you your *sample*. Can you tell right away?"

"No, Abu-Khan. I'll need to find someone with access to lab equipment. I'll need to take it to a doctor. Can you get me an appointment with one?"

"No. No one can know this request is coming from me."

"I see. Yes, of course. But can you give me the name of a doctor? Can you find one who specializes in infertility?"

He winced when she said the word *infertility*. "No. My secretaries would normally get information like that for me, but I can't ask them about *this*."

"Okay then. I'll find a doctor myself. Get me a sample and let me know when it's ready. I'll find a

11

doctor to analyze it."

"Fine," he said with the whining inflection of a thirteen-year-old. He obviously wasn't used to being told what to do.

She explained he had to ejaculate into a clean glass container and the sample had to be taken to the lab immediately after it was produced.

"Where am I supposed to get a glass container? How will I know if it's clean enough?"

Layla agreed to find and prepare a container. "I'll leave it with Omid," she said.

"No." The alarm on his face suggested she'd threatened to take the sample from his body herself—with a knife. "No one can know about this."

"Okay. When I get the container, I'll ask to see you."

She smiled as she headed downstairs to ask the kitchen workers for a jar. Apparently this man could run a country, but that might be the only thing he could do.

Two hours later, Abu-Khan handed the jam jar back to her, carefully wrapped in the folds of a silk scarf. Pulling aside the cloth, she saw it now contained a puddle of milky goo. The royal essence.

He shifted from one foot to the other. "Don't forget: no one can know this came from me."

"Right. So what should I say to the doctor?"

"Tell him it's your husband's. Tell him your husband doesn't want to come in himself."

"Okay. I can do that. If I try really hard, I can conceive of a Behruzi male being embarrassed about this subject." She waited for Abu-Khan to laugh, but he hadn't noticed her sarcasm. She asked if he could provide a driver.

"Oh. I hadn't thought of that." He rubbed the back of his neck. "No, I don't think I should. I don't want anyone to know."

"Okay. I'll take a taxi. But I haven't had a chance to change any money."

"A taxi? Money?" It was possible Abu-Khan had never been in a taxi in his life. "How much will you need? I think I have some cash here." He rummaged through the contents of the bottom drawer of his desk and took out a small box.

"I don't know. How much are taxis?"

"I have no idea. But here, this should be enough." He pulled a wad of bills from the box and handed it to her.

"Okay. I'll return whatever's left over when I get back."

"That won't be necessary." A few minutes later she stood on the sidewalk a block from the palace, with a chador covering all but her face, looking for a taxi. She was in Behruz. Really in Behruz. Not just in the palace. On the street. Memories came flooding back to her. Never mind the crazy nature of her mission; she was in the country of her childhood. She smiled at everyone who passed her.

She flagged down a taxi.

"Take me to an obstetrician please," she said to the driver.

"A what?"

"An obstetrician. A doctor who specializes in pregnancy and childbirth."

"Excuse me, khanoum, I don't know of such a doctor in Behruz City. Women go to the general hospital when they need to see a doctor about *such matters*." He whispered the last two words.

Her mother had told her about the general hospital in Behruz City. It was the largest hospital in the country, the place where the poor went for treatment. She didn't think they'd be equipped to deal with infertility. They probably couldn't deal with *anything* fast enough for her needs. It might take hours to be seen, and she didn't have hours. The sperm in her pocket would be losing motility within an hour.

"No, I don't want the general hospital. Take me to a private doctor."

"What doctor, khanoum?" the man asked.

"Any doctor. Not too near the palace. A good doctor if you know of one."

He glanced at her over his shoulder, his eyebrows raised in question. "Any doctor?"

"Yes, please. And hurry."

Chapter Two

Majid ate his afternoon meal at his desk, as usual. It was rice and lamb prepared by Mohammed, an old man who cooked over charcoal embers at a stand in front of Majid's clinic. When he finished eating, Majid stepped out into the reception area to see if any of his afternoon patients had arrived. One woman sat alone in the room, not wearing a chador. The letters *UCLA* were written across the back of her T-shirt. An American? He couldn't see her face—she was turned toward the window—but her hair was a shade lighter than was typical in Behruz, and it was pulled back into a ponytail. A chador hung from the chair next to hers, so apparently she'd been wearing one when she came in.

His receptionist, Saba, whispered to him, "She doesn't have an appointment, but she says she needs to see you urgently."

The woman turned toward them and stood. The details of her appearance—tall, almost as tall as he was, slender, small breasts, pert nose, big round eyes the color of rich chocolate, thick lashes, and lush, full lips—all seemed to be revealed in slow motion.

She stepped toward him with her hand extended. Definitely not Behruzi. A Behruzi woman wouldn't offer her hand to a man who wasn't part of her family. He took the hand in his. It was soft and warm and *feminine*. She smelled like lilacs.

"Hi," she said in English but then she switched to Farsi. "My name is Layla Shirvani. I have a semen sample I'd like to have analyzed." She pulled a small jar from her pocket. "Can you do that? Do you have a microscope?"

What? A semen sample? No one had ever walked into his clinic with a semen sample before. "How do you do, Mrs. Shirvani. I am Doctor Majid Nassiri. I'm sorry, but this is rather irregular. The sample would need to be deposited in a sterile container, and it would have to be produced here so I could analyze it right away."

"I know this is a little unorthodox. I'm a certified nurse-midwife in the States. I sterilized the jar myself, and the sample was produced about thirty minutes ago. Please, I hope you can analyze it without having my, uh, *husband* come in. He's embarrassed about this." Her head tilted to the side, and she smiled an irresistible appeal. "Please?"

"Okay. I guess I could take a look."

"Thank you." Her smile widened.

"You can wait here. This won't take long."

"Oh please, I'd like to watch if you don't mind." That adorable smile still lit her face.

"All right." His voice came out gruff. Saba was watching him curiously. He'd never invited a patient into the lab before.

She walked ahead of him, moving in that casual way American women had, swinging her arms loosely and looking at everything. Her lilac scent drifted back to him, making him feel lightheaded.

She hovered near him while he prepared the sample, seeming to want to grab the materials from his hands and do it herself.

He placed the slide under the microscope. "I went to medical school at the University of Minnesota and did my internship there too. We had certified nurse-midwives in the hospital where I worked."

"Oh, then you know what we do. Most people don't."

"I have a lot of respect for what you do, actually. I know we doctors sometimes make the process of birth more complicated than it needs to be."

He bent over the microscope and turned the dial to bring the sample into focus. She stood right behind him, practically "breathing down his neck." A shimmering tingle coursed through him as he imagined what it would be like to literally have her breath on his neck. Or any other part on his body.

He stood. She had her hands flattened together as if in prayer in front of her lips, waiting for his evaluation.

"The count is low, but the sperm look healthy. With a little help getting them into the right place at the right time, conception should be possible."

"Can I see?" she asked.

There was no reason why she shouldn't. He moved aside, and she bent over the microscope. His eyes trailed along the bumps of her vertebrae, which were clearly outlined through the fabric of her T-shirt, to her nicely rounded bottom…

He pulled his eyes away from that nicely rounded bottom. She was a patient, after all.

She stood up from the microscope, her eyes gleaming. "They're active little swimmers, aren't they?" This was obviously very good news. His chest filled with pride, as if he'd engineered her husband's sperm motility himself rather than just reporting it. An image came to him of her with a swollen belly. The man who would be sharing the excitement of pregnancy with her was a lucky guy.

He told her that the more sophisticated procedures used in modern fertility treatment weren't available in Behruz. "Some couples go to India for treatment, but perhaps in your case the U.S. would be the best option."

The light disappeared from her eyes in an instant. "Oh no, I won't be going to the States or India for this. My husband can't leave because…" She cleared her throat. "Because of his work."

"I see," Majid said, but he didn't see at all. This husband of hers didn't seem very interested in getting his wife pregnant. "What is his work—if you don't mind my asking?"

She tilted her head down and mumbled, "I don't think he wants me talking about it."

"Of course. Please excuse me. I didn't mean to pry."

She looked up. "You have no reason to apologize. It was a natural question. I'm the one who should be embarrassed. It's just that my husband is very secretive."

"Say no more." Majid felt terrible for adding to her discomfort. What an oaf the husband must be.

"How about artificial insemination?" she asked.

"Yes, of course. That would be a fairly easy thing to try." They discussed the situation and agreed on a plan that involved injecting sperm directly into the uterus to increase the chance of success. They'd both heard of a process that would "wash" the semen to select and concentrate the healthiest sperm, but neither knew exactly what the process entailed.

"I'll read up on it and ask around," Majid said. "I know of one lab that may be able to do it. Where are you in your menstrual cycle?"

Her eyes darted around the room and then settled on the floor in front of her. What had come over her? She'd seemed comfortable discussing aspects of fertility a minute ago, but now she was suddenly timid?

"I'm not sure," she stammered. "I'd have to check. That is, I've just come from the States a few days ago, and I'm still jet-lagged. My cycle may be disrupted."

"Okay." He didn't think travel would normally upset a cycle that much, but maybe for her it did. "If you decide you want to proceed and you want me to help, let me know."

"Yes, I will. As soon as I know what my husband wants to do." She started to stretch open the chador, but she didn't put it on. "I have one more question—"

"Of course. What is it?"

"Was I supposed to wear this thing while I was with you?" She indicated the chador in her hands.

Majid had been prepared for a medical question, not a question about chador etiquette. How long had she been in the country? What she'd told him about herself didn't add up. She was married to a Behruzi who couldn't leave the country because of his work, and they'd been married long enough to be facing a struggle with fertility, yet she didn't know such a basic thing as when to wear a chador?

He didn't consider himself to be the best source of information on the subject, but he answered as best he could. "Most women do wear a chador in the waiting room and when they first talk to me, but of course they end up removing it if I examine them. They usually have a husband with them in that case. However, Western women often come in without one. Some have simply never adopted the custom of wearing them. Others wear them on the street but take them off when they're inside. There are no hard and fast rules. You can do what feels comfortable to you."

She listened to all that with her mouth set in determined concentration. "Okay, thanks. This is going to take some getting used to."

She pulled the chador over her head. It looked a little comical: too short and hanging longer on one side than the other, but he didn't say anything. It was good enough.

Back in the waiting room, where two patients now waited to be seen, Saba eyed Majid with speculation and accusation in her eyes. It wasn't like him to let a drop-in patient put him behind in his schedule.

Mrs. Shirvani was opening her billfold.

"There's no charge," Majid said.

She shoved the billfold into a pocket of her jeans and smiled. "Thank you."

"You're welcome. As I said, let me know if you want any more assistance." He handed her his card.

She stuffed it into her pocket along with the billfold. "All right. I'll let you know when I find out what my husband wants to do."

She walked out the door wearing the lopsided chador. Would he see her again?

****

The smell of spices and meat greeted Layla when she stepped out of Dr. Nassiri's clinic. An old man in a turban was preparing food at a stand on the sidewalk.

Her heart swelled with a sense of homecoming.

The taxi had only cost the equivalent of about three dollars—she had plenty of money left—but she decided to walk back to the palace. She seemed to skim along the sidewalk, happy expectation bubbling inside her chador cocoon. She was in Behruz. The sky was dazzling bright, and she had good news for Abu-Khan.

She reviewed what she'd told Dr. Nassiri and tried to figure out a way to reconcile it with her actual circumstances. It seemed impossible. She should just find a new doctor to help with the insemination—that would be easier than trying to manage the lies she'd just told—but she didn't want a new doctor. There was something about Dr. Nassiri—and it wasn't just that he was handsome—although she had to admit that was part of it. He wasn't handsome in the classic sense, not like Dan. And he wasn't muscular like Dan; he was more *lanky* and scholarly looking. But, oh, his eyes. They were kind and knowing and ringed by thick lashes. They were deep and dark with depths of sensuality masked behind reserve. The kind of eyes you just wanted to drown in.

Not that she'd really noticed his eyes.

One step at a time. Let him find a lab that could prepare the sperm. Then she'd figure out what to do next.

Meanwhile, the thrill of being back in the land of her childhood echoed through her. Her heart remembered when these streets were home. She greeted a smartly dressed businessman coming out of an office building and a woman sweeping the sidewalk in front of her shop. The woman was wearing high heels under her chador and neatly pressed jeans. Layla bought chocolate in a little store that sold snack foods and magazines. She smiled at an old man leading a donkey down the street.

She smiled when she thought of Dr. Nassiri's handsome, dark eyes.

She went into a stationery shop and asked the woman behind the counter, "Can you tell me how to get to the sultan's palace?" The woman pointed the way and started explaining, but her directions were too complicated to follow. "Never mind. I'll just head that way and then ask again after a few blocks."

Everyone returned her greeting in a friendly way but with questions in their eyes. Maybe she wasn't supposed to be saying "hello" to strangers in Behruz.

She hadn't thought how she was going to get back *into* the palace, but apparently Abu-Khan had. The soldiers in the guard station welcomed her back, and one of them escorted her to Abu-Khan's office.

Abu-Khan looked up sharply. "What took so long?"

His scowl couldn't dampen her happy spirits. "It was such a beautiful day, and I was anxious to see the city, so I walked back."

"Dressed like that? Didn't your mother explain that you need to wear a chador?"

Layla indicated the chador draped over her arm. "Yes, she did. I wore it until I got back to the palace."

"Good. I hope Mary also explained that you're not to go around shaking hands with everyone you meet. It's inappropriate for you to touch a man you're not related to."

"Yes, of course. I know that." Her mother had told her, but she'd forgotten. Had Dr. Nassiri thought her brazen when she reached out to shake his hand? Maybe not. Hopefully not. He'd spent enough time in the States to understand American ways.

"Good. Now tell me, did you find a doctor?"

Layla told him that conception did seem possible, and she explained the process of intrauterine insemination. "You realize, of course, we can't do this without Mina's knowledge. You'll have to explain it to her."

Abu-Khan's eyes flew open. "Uh, no, *you'll* have to explain it."

Layla bristled. This guy wasn't *her* sultan. She didn't want him thinking he could dictate her actions, but actually it made sense for her to be the one to tell Mina. She could imagine Abu-Khan stammering through a garbled explanation of artificial insemination. Anyway, she wanted to talk privately with Mina. The girl was marrying a man more than twice her age. Had she had any choice? Probably not. It would be pretty hard to say no to the sultan of the country. The girl might be a virgin. She might not know what she was getting into.

Layla would watch to see if Mina needed the support of someone who wasn't in awe of Abu-Khan's power. And she would find out about Mina's menstrual cycle so she could report back to Doctor Nassiri.

The two young women met in the palace courtyard the next day. Mina gave the traditional greeting in Farsi, "*Salaam*, Layla, I hope you are well."

Layla gave the obligatory response, "Salaam. I am well, thank you. How are you?"

And Mina completed the ritual. "I am well, thank you."

They kissed each other on the cheek.

They sat on a bench surrounded by rose bushes, looking out over a lush lawn to the high brick wall that surrounded the palace. Mina removed her chador, revealing a tight coral-colored T-shirt and expensive-looking jeans. Petite and with delicate features, she looked like a child playing grownup—with her hair piled up on the top of her head in an elaborate coif and with a heavy application of lipstick, mascara, and eyeliner. Still, she seemed innocent and sweet; it was easy to see why Abu-Khan was smitten with her.

"Thank you for taking the time to see me," Layla said. "You must be busy getting ready for the wedding."

"I don't have much to do, actually. Abu-Khan is taking care of everything. And I'm glad to get a chance to know you." She took Layla's hand. "I really appreciate your taking the time to meet with me."

They made more small talk, and then Layla got to the point of the meeting. "Abu-Khan has asked me to talk to you about something."

Mina's eyes grew large. "That sounds interesting. Or ominous."

"It's a bit delicate, actually. He wants me to tell you about certain issues that might affect his ability to give you a baby."

"Oh. I was wondering about that. I know neither of his first two wives got pregnant, but then his American wife did have a baby, so I was thinking maybe everything was all right."

This was going well. The girl wasn't entirely naïve on the subject. "Although there was the one baby, conception is still unlikely without a little help from modern medicine. Is it important to you to have a child?"

"Yes, very much so," the girl replied. "It will be my duty to have children for the royal succession, but I want them anyway. I hope it will be possible." There was pleading in her eyes. "What kind of 'help' are you talking about?"

Layla explained how artificial insemination, using Abu-Khan's sperm, would increase the chances of conception significantly.

Mina said, "Great. What do I have to do? When do we start?"

Layla asked the girl about her menstrual cycle.

"That's easy," Mina said. "I got my period three days ago." She studied a calendar app on her cell phone and added, "They come every twenty-eight days, always the same."

"Great. The fact that you're regular will make it easier to predict the time of ovulation."

Layla calculated they would be performing the insemination in about eleven days, shortly after the newlyweds returned from their honeymoon trip to the Summer Palace in eastern Behruz—unless Abu-Khan wanted to wait.

Mina was grinning. "As far as I'm concerned, the sooner the better."

"You do understand that Abu-Khan is a little uncomfortable with this," Layla said. "He doesn't want anyone to know."

"Oh, of course. I won't tell a soul, not even my mother. He's going to be my husband. I'll be 200% perfectly loyal to him in every way."

Layla appreciated the girl's fervor. "Do you have

any questions about marriage? About the sexual aspects of marriage?"

Mina didn't hesitate in answering. "I don't think so." There was no one in sight except for soldiers at the guard station across the lawn, but still she moved closer and spoke softly. "Are you wondering if I'm a virgin? Did Abu-Khan ask you to find out? I am. I saved myself for my husband, I promise."

The girl was surprisingly forthright. "Well, that's nice. No, Abu-Khan did not ask me to check. I just wanted to be sure you knew what to expect on your wedding night."

Mina's lips stretched into a confident smile. "I lived with an aunt and uncle in France for a year after high school. Their kids showed me some videos, so I think I'm prepared. The smile grew suggestive.

Mina was apparently going to be an eager bride.

Layla called Dan that evening. He was disoriented at first—he'd been asleep—but he was soon wide awake.

"How's it going, kiddo?" he asked, using the nickname he'd used since she was a child. "Are you having fun?"

Fun? Not really. The visit wasn't *fun*, not like a trip to Disneyland or a vacation at the beach, but it was satisfying a longing in her, one so vague and deep she couldn't name it. From the moment she first glimpsed Behruz City from the air, she'd felt a sense of *coming home*.

But she gave Dan the expected answer. Yes, she was having fun. She started to tell him about the boring dinners and about the sweetness of the bride-to-be, but he was too excited about his own news to listen. He was in *Dallas*, working as a college football coach. His *dream job*. His team had won their first game thirteen to six.

She stretched out on the bed, happy to hear the enthusiasm in his voice.

"Wait until you see the stadium," he said. "It holds twelve thousand people. And the cheerleading squad is amazing. You won't believe their costumes. The coach is great; she used to be a Dallas Cowboys cheerleader. You'll see everything when you get here. How much longer are you going to be in Behruz?"

"I've only been here five days. I'll be back in three and a half weeks."

"Can't you get here sooner? You're expected to take a leadership role in the faculty wives' booster club. They're making plans without you, and that's not good."

"September twenty-ninth, Dan. I told you that before I left."

"Right. Can you come straight here? There's a dinner with the dean, the athletic director, and the other coaches and their wives on October $2^{nd}$. It's really important that you be here."

"No, Dan. I can't fly straight there. It would cost a fortune to change my reservation. It'll be cheaper to fly home and then go from San Francisco to Dallas."

What a nightmare that was going to be. She hadn't completely recovered from the trip *to* Behruz, and the return would be just as exhausting. Yet she'd just agreed to fly to Dallas two days after she got home.

Dan told her to be sure to bring her mauve dress. He thought it would give just the impression of maturity and beauty he'd like his new coworkers to see.

He said he didn't want her looking "like some kind of *hippie*." He was worried one of her flights might be delayed. She promised to bring the dress he liked, but she couldn't make any guarantees about the airline schedule.

He talked about the game his team would be playing that weekend, about the strengths and weaknesses of the various players and the plays he planned to use. Then suddenly he interrupted himself. "Well, darlin', it's time for me to get ready for work."

"I miss you; I love you," she said. "Good luck with the game."

"I love you too, kiddo."

She had that reassurance with her, tucked into her heart, when she slid into the softness of her huge bed. Dan missed her. He loved her. He wanted her with him.

She thought about the unexpected pleasure of finding she was needed here. Abu-Khan and Mina were pinning their hopes of having a baby on her.

They were both such paradoxes: he with his arrogance and vulnerability and she with her sweetness and her surprising savvy. Dr. Nassiri was a man of contradictions too. He was gravely serious and yet had that restless fire in his eyes. Those eyes and that fire haunted her as she drifted off to sleep.

Chapter Three

Majid was sitting at his desk, trying to decide what to do about a patient whose labor was stalled when Saba buzzed to tell him Khanoum Shirvani was there to see him. "Send her back to my office," he told the receptionist.

He quickly cleared some of the clutter off his desk and straightened his tie, and then he berated himself for his reaction. She was a patient, he reminded himself. He was her doctor. And she was married.

She breezed into his office, wearing her chador this time. She removed it, revealing a T-shirt with letters across the front that proclaimed *Midwife at your cervix*. He laughed. Humor overtook both worry about the patient and his unsettling reaction to seeing her again. She looked confused. Then she followed his eyes and realized he was laughing at the words stretched across her bosom. She smiled.

That unselfconscious smile.

He reminded himself: she was a patient; he was her doctor; she was an American, *and she was married*.

"I was wondering if you were able to find a lab to prepare the semen," she said.

"Yes, I did. There's one not far from here that's done it half a dozen times."

"Great. Do you happen to know if there are ovulation predictor kits available in Behruz City?"

"Yes." He wrote the name and address of a pharmacy on a piece of notebook paper and handed it to her. "This is our most modern pharmacy. I'm sure they have it. It'll be a urine-based test. Will you know how to use it?"

"I should be able to figure it out."

"All right then. Let me know if you want any assistance."

She folded the paper and put it in the pocket of her jeans. "I'll have to think about it. My husband still doesn't want to come in."

Majid couldn't suppress a scowl. He was beginning to doubt the man seriously cared about having a child with Layla. "I guess he could do his part at home, as long as you understand the need for speed."

A glimmer of enthusiasm lit her eyes. "Yes, that might work."

Something about that glimmer made him think of her as a woman, not a patient, and he remembered he needed to caution her about one point. "You and your husband should abstain from sex for at least two days before he produces the sample. There will be more sperm after a little abstinence."

"Uh..." Her head turned down. She mumbled, "Okay." Fury flashed through Majid. Was a few days abstinence too much to ask of the man? This husband of hers didn't deserve the thrill of sharing a pregnancy with her.

"Thank you, Dr. Nassiri." She reached for her chador, preparing to cover up that ridiculous T-shirt and leave.

"Wait. I hate to ask this, but I wonder if you could help me with one of my patients." He didn't want her to leave, and he really did need help.

It took her a moment to register what he was asking. "Sure. What's the problem?"

"The young woman came in with her husband about two hours ago. Usually there would be a mother or mother-in-law with her, but they're from southern Behruz, and they have no family here. It sounds like she was in active labor before they came in, but she was no longer contracting when they got here and I haven't been able to examine her."

"What do you mean—you haven't been able to examine her?"

He rubbed the back of his neck. "It's a common problem in this country. She won't let me touch her. She's timid and modest and scared to death. There's a good chance that coming here and facing me is what stopped her labor. I've called for a nurse to come in, but she won't be here for another hour or two."

"Do you want me to check her?"

"That would be helpful if you can do it without upsetting her, but the main thing is to explain what's happening—she probably doesn't have a clue—and help her relax. I can manage the labor without checking her if I have to. I've done it before."

Layla nodded. "Okay, I can do that. What's her name? Where is she?"

Majid led her to the labor room and introduced her to the patient, Nida, and her husband, Hamid. He showed Layla where she could find supplies and then waited a few minutes to see how the girl responded to having a newcomer in the room. When he saw Nida relaxing into Layla's touch and listening with quiet attention to Layla's reassuring words, he left to attend to other patients.

An hour later, when he returned to the labor room, he found Nida was now wearing a gown and sitting on a low stool. Layla sat behind her, massaging her shoulders. Nida's husband sat on a folding chair in the corner of the room, slightly more relaxed but with an appeal on his face that screamed *save me*. Nida moaned a low, active-labor moan while Layla murmured encouraging words. "You're doing great, Nida. That's it. Keep breathing, nice and slow. Yes. That's it. You're doing great."

Layla glanced up at Majid and smiled an angelic smile. What it must be like to be the husband who got to bathe in that smile every day. She held up seven fingers and mouthed the words, "seven centimeters." Then she turned her attention back to Nida. Watching Layla's hands move over the girl's back, he could imagine what it would feel like to have those graceful fingers sweeping across *his* back. He stifled that image. He repeated his mantra: *she's a patient; she's married.* He listened to her voice, reassuring, coaxing, *loving.*

"You're doing beautifully, Nida. It won't be long now. The doctor is here." Nida glanced at him and then went back to her bent-over laboring position. "He asked me to sit with you for a while because he could see how scary this is for you, but I'm not going to deliver the baby; he is. He really wants to help you."

The girl stiffened for a second, but then she had to concentrate on breathing her way through another contraction. Layla resumed her litany of encouraging words.

When the contraction ended, Nida stretched up and turned to ask Layla over her shoulder. "Can you stay?"

Layla turned to him for his reaction. He nodded.

She said to Nida, "Yes, I can stay. I'd love to be with you for the birth of your baby."

\*\*\*\*

Layla excused herself and went into the hallway to call Omid.

"Where are you, khanoum?" Omid asked. "Abu-Khan has been asking for you."

"Tell him I'm helping a woman in labor."

Omid was silent for a moment, probably dreading having to relay her message to Abu-Khan. "When will you be back?"

"I have no idea. A woman is *in labor*. The baby could be born in an hour or two or it could take all night."

"All night?"

"Yes, Omid. Tell the guards I may be late."

"But khanoum, there is a special dinner tonight. Abu-Khan..."

"I may be *very* late. Please tell Abu-Khan. Thank you, Omid." She hung up thinking that if Abu-Khan didn't like her missing one of his dinners, he could deport her.

The conversation reminded her of Dan's complaints about the long and unpredictable hours of her work. During the month they were together before he left for Dallas, she missed two dates with him because of labors that dragged on into the night. One was to an important Giants' baseball game. Dan had been excited about the game: he'd pulled some strings to get special behind-the-dugout seats. She kept calling him all day to say she thought the baby would be born "soon," but the labor dragged on and on. How stressful it had been—wanting to give all her attention to the laboring woman but at the same time feeling guilty for disrupting Dan's plans. The midwife in her knew that what was needed was patience, but the woman in her— the woman who wanted to please Dan—kept hoping the baby would hurry up and be born.

Dan arrived late to the game and watched it alone with an empty seat beside him.

She apologized and pleaded for his understanding. For permission to be committed to the work she loved.

It felt good now to have stood her ground with Omid: to have simply told him what she needed to do. What she *wanted* to do. She should be more assertive with Dan.

When she returned to the labor room, Majid left to attend to his other patients. Layla worked hard for the next hour as Nida sailed through transition. She breathed with Nida and moaned with her and massaged her and hugged her and praised and encouraged her. Hamid stayed resolutely in his chair in the corner, resisting all Layla's efforts to involve him.

The nurse arrived. She was a starchy, bird-like woman, probably in her early twenties. She set up the equipment that would be needed for delivery, glancing at Nida and Layla now and then and somehow managing to convey disapproval. It wasn't clear what exactly was the source of her disapproval. Maybe Nida for moaning her pain, maybe Layla for encouraging her, or maybe labor in general.

Dr. Nassiri attended to other patients while Layla watched over Nida. The nurse let him know when the baby's head was first visible, and he came back into the room. He pulled a sterile gown on over his clothes, washed his hands, put on gloves, and got into position to catch the baby.

Layla asked Hamid, "Would you like to watch your baby be born?"

His eyes darted around the room as if he expected it to appear from behind some piece of equipment. "What? Now?"

She said, "Yes, now," and nudged him into position behind Dr. Nassiri. He kept his eyes averted, his whole body in a clench.

At just the right moment, when the head was about to emerge, she told him, with her teacher's authority in her voice, "Look now."

He did. The fear in his eyes turned to disbelief and then hope and then fear again as a wrinkled, gooey baby boy slid into Dr. Nassiri's hands.

Even though she'd held more than a thousand babies as they made this transition—from warm water to cold air, from soft, confining tissue to open space—Layla held her breath, and no doubt Hamid did too. The baby had a new, urgent job to do—take air into his lungs—and he had to learn it quickly.

Dr. Nassiri brushed a towel across the wrinkled, wet face, and the baby reacted. He stiffened and gulped in air and cried out his indignation. Layla gulped in air too as Dr. Nassiri placed the baby on Nida's belly and the nurse reached to help support him.

Layla smiled reassurance at Hamid and said, "Congratulations."

Tears streamed down the new father's face.

Forty-five minutes later, Layla and Dr. Nassiri left Nida and Hamid cooing to each other and to their baby. Dr. Nassiri explained that the nurse would stay with

Nida through the night.

They sat in his office across the cluttered desk from each other, drinking hot tea left for them by Saba. For once Layla didn't mind the over-sweetness of Behruzi tea. She held the cup in front of her lips, inhaling the aromatic steam.

He said, "Thank you."

"It was a pleasure. It was a lovely birth."

"I can pay you, but not what you'd make in the States."

"Oh no, I was glad to do it. I liked supporting Nida without having any other responsibilities at all."

"You were an enormous help."

"As I said, it was a pleasure."

He looked at his watch. "It's after eight. I'm sorry to have kept you so late. I hope your husband won't be upset."

She'd forgotten about her supposed husband, and she'd forgotten Abu-Khan too. He probably would be upset, but that wasn't *her* problem. "I suppose you think a good little Behruzi wife should be more concerned about the possibility of upsetting her husband, so I should tell you—I'm not a good little Behruzi wife. I'm really more American than Behruzi."

Dr. Nassiri gave a wry smile. "I'd noticed that. Still, there's your name and the fact that you speak Farsi so well…" They were speaking English now, but they'd used Farsi while they were with Nida.

"My father was Behruzi, but my mother American. They lived here after they were married, until I was seven, but then my dad died and my mom took me and my brother and sisters to live in California. We kids spoke Farsi at home even after we moved, and we always had Farsi-speaking friends—Iranian and Afghani as well as Behruzi—so I never forgot my father's language."

"I see. Have you been back here before?"

"No. This is the first time I've been back since my father died."

"And your husband? Is he Behruzi?"

Oh crap. This fib was becoming totally unwieldy.

"There's something I need to tell you," she said.

"Yes?" he asked, all attention, all doctorly kindness.

"This is embarrassing."

He reached toward her as if to place his hand over hers, but his hand stopped in mid-air. He picked up a pen and tapped it on the desk. "You know you can tell me anything, Mrs. Shirvani. I'm a doctor."

"I think you could call me Layla, don't you?"

He colored slightly. He tapped the pen on the desk three times. "Yes, of course, and you must call me Majid."

"Good. That's out of the way. Now... Well, this is ridiculous. I'm just going to say it." She looked directly into his eyes. "The semen sample I brought isn't my husband's."

"What?"

"That is, I don't have a husband." There. She'd said it.

"You're not married? But..."

What must he be thinking?

She explained that the sample she'd brought was from an uncle who was, like the fictional husband, determined not to let anyone know he had a fertility problem. "I'm sorry I lied. My uncle suggested I say the sample was my husband's. It didn't sound like a bad idea when he came up with it, but it got complicated very quickly."

"What were you going to do when it came time for the insemination?"

She laughed. "That was one of the complications."

"Hmmm." Tap, tap, tap went the pen. "I know there are men in this country who would be as uncomfortable with this problem as your uncle appears to be, but I did find it hard to believe that *you* would be married to one of them."

"Well, I'm not. I'm not married to anyone. I am engaged, however, to a nice American."

"Oh, I see."

She told him she'd come to Behruz for an uncle's wedding, implying there were two uncles, the one with the fertility problem—she was staying with him and his wife—and another one who was getting married. Another fib, or maybe *distortion* was more accurate, and a pretty major omission of the fact that the uncle she was staying with happened to be the sultan of the country, but at least Majid no longer thought *she* was the one who needed sperm injected into her uterus. "I'm hoping for quick results," she said. "I'm only going to be here three more weeks, and I'd really like to see success before I leave."

"How long have they been trying?" Majid asked.

Ha. Abu-Khan and Mina hadn't even had sex yet. "Not long, but he's been married before, more than once, and none of his wives became pregnant, so he has reason to suspect there's a problem."

"Is the wife as reticent as he is?"

"No. She's amazingly comfortable with the

process."

"How old is she?"

"I didn't ask, but I'd say she's in her early twenties."

"Good. Her being young will increase their chances of success." He took a deep breath and smiled his warm doctor smile. "So you're not married."

"Nope." Somehow the word came out a little too exuberantly cheerful. "But I am engaged," she reminded him—and herself. Still she felt *unencumbered.*

Majid was still smiling—with his lips and his eyes and really his whole face. "You don't wear a ring?"

"Oh." They both stared at her bare hands, which were clasped together on the desk. "No. I left it at home. I didn't want to wear it while I'm traveling, you know, in case something should happen to it."

\*\*\*\*

Majid couldn't take his eyes away from those hands. Those long, graceful fingers and the nails, which were short, unpainted, and neatly trimmed. His mother wore her nails long and polished, as did his sisters and aunts. Every woman he knew did, except for the poorest of his patients. But not Layla. That was the thing about her. She was natural. There was no strain and effort in her. She seemed somehow *exposed*, not hiding anything or covering anything. It made him feel he should protect her.

He remembered when he'd briefly grasped her hand the day they met. It had been soft and smooth. And naked. He had an urge to reach for it again.

He was relieved he wouldn't have to ask her to spread those long legs before him for a clinical procedure. But for some reason he liked the idea of her being engaged to "a nice American" even less than the idea of her being married to an uptight Behruzi. He didn't like thinking of her with the nice American at all.

"Your fiancé didn't come with you?"

She laughed. "No. He had no interest in a visit to Behruz. He's a football coach. He just started a new job at a college in Texas, so this is a busy time for him. You know, the start of the season."

That was even worse. The "nice American" was a football coach. Majid pictured the man: tall, probably blond, and built like an athlete. Majid might be considered tall, but his hair and eyes were dark and he was built like a doctor. Like a healthy doctor, to be sure, one who worked out whenever he got a chance and played soccer occasionally, but still—not like an athlete at all.

"Is your fiancé by any chance blond?" he asked, and then he immediately regretted it. What a stupid, irrelevant question.

She said *yes* as if it were a normal thing to ask.

His stomach rumbled, and he realized he hadn't eaten since breakfast. She probably hadn't either. "I'm sorry. I haven't offered you anything to eat all afternoon. Are you hungry? Can I get you dinner?"

She said she was starving and would love dinner. "But don't you have to stay to be sure Nida is stable?"

"Yes, I do. But I can bring dinner to us. Wait here." He left and returned ten minutes later with chicken kebabs, rice, and fresh flatbread. "This was prepared by one of the finest chefs in Behruz City, the street vendor from in front of my office. He even had a fork for you."

He produced the plastic fork and watched her use it

to slide hunks of chicken off the wooden skewer. He used a piece of bread to do the same thing. "You were magnificent helping that girl," he said.

She speared a piece of chicken with her fork. "Helping women in labor is a sacred experience for me. I lose myself in it."

"Yes, I can see that." Watching her work with Nida had reawakened his own feelings of reverence for childbirth. "When is your uncle's wedding going to take place?"

"On Friday," she replied.

"Our sultan is also getting married on Friday."

"So I heard." She slipped the piece of chicken into her mouth and drove her fork into the mound of rice.

Majid poured more tea from the thermos into her cup. "You must have a million things to do to get ready. I'm sorry I tied you up all afternoon."

"Actually, I'm not busy at all, except for attending formal dinners. There doesn't seem to be much I can do to help with the wedding."

He hesitated to ask, but she was the perfect person to assist with his project. He couldn't resist. "What about afterward? Will you be busy next week?"

"I have nothing planned for after the wedding. I suppose I'll explore the city. Frankly, I'll be glad when we're done with the dinners."

Majid chuckled. "I can imagine. I know what the lead-up to a Behruzi wedding is like. The reason I asked is that I was wondering if you'd have time to help with a project I'm working on."

Interest glinted in her eyes. "What do you have in mind?"

"The project involves maternity care at the general

41

hospital here in Behruz City. I'm on staff there. My hope is to provide support for women in labor. Patients aren't allowed to have family members with them, and the nurses are too busy to give personal attention, so women end up going through labor alone. Nida would almost certainly have ended up with a cesarean if she'd had her baby there. With no one to help her relax, she wouldn't have been able to ease into labor, and she wouldn't have been able to handle the pain."

"Why can't they have family members with them?"

"First of all, doctors think it would be a big nuisance. Secondly, even if the doctors did support the idea, the labor ward is too small; there's no way we could maintain privacy for the other patients if family members were present. So I'm trying to institute a program that would provide services like doulas provide in your country. The hospital would train and pay non-medical women to stay with labor patients, help them with breathing and other coping techniques, and encourage them. They'd do what you did for Nida today—minus the vaginal check, of course."

"It's a wonderful idea. Other developing countries have done it, and the results have been impressive: fewer complications, fewer cesareans, and fewer deaths. How far along are you in the project?"

Majid laughed. "At the hoping-to-get-some-money-to-fund-it stage. Behruz hasn't met the World Health Organization's millennial goals for maternity care. We're not even close. I'm applying for a grant from a foundation in your country that wants to help countries like us improve maternity care. I was wondering if you'd be interested in helping."

Her eyes shimmered with excitement. "I'd love to.

Is there anything I can do in the short time I'll be here?"

Her enthusiasm made him even more excited about the idea himself. Something quickened in his heart: something that had been missing from his life. Comradery. With someone who shared his experience and values.

He explained that before he could apply for the grant he had to get the Behruzi Health Department to commit to paying part of the ongoing expenses. That was where he thought she might help.

"Okay, what can I do?"

"The first hurdle is to get some of the hospital staff on board with the project. The other doctors are skeptical that something so non-medical could make a difference. I'd like to demonstrate the value of labor support. That's where you come in. I was wondering if you'd have time to do a little doula work in the hospital next week."

She smiled her soft smile. "I'd love to."

"Great. You'll be paid, of course. The U.S. foundation has approved funds to finance this phase."

"Oh really, that won't be necessary."

"Yes it is." He suggested that the foundation could send the payment to her home in San Francisco, and she gave him her mother's address.

He told her about the doctors she might meet while she was there: one who was still a big fan of episiotomies, one who had a particularly high rate of cesareans, and the head of the department, Dr. Mansur, who was the most resistant to the idea of the doula project.

"Those are all men. Don't you have any female doctors?"

"No. There are some in other departments of the hospital, but at the moment there aren't any in Obstetrics. I hesitate to tell you why."

She raised her eyebrows, waiting.

He could imagine how she'd react when he told her. "It's because the head of the department doesn't think women can do the job."

He'd thought she would be offended, but she just laughed. She muttered so softly he could barely hear, "Would that be because penises and adam's apples are so very useful in the practice of medicine?"

She was outrageous.

She was also, apparently, embarrassed by her own outrageousness. She clenched her eyes shut and shook her head. "I'm sorry. I can't believe I said that. It's something my midwife friend Roxanne says when we encounter chauvinism in our work back home. I have to learn to watch my tongue."

They'd finished eating. He dropped their plates into a wastebasket under his desk.

"I don't believe I've ever heard a woman utter that word before."

"What word? You mean *penis*?"

"Yes, that one."

She grinned. She must think his discomfort was amusing. "You didn't even hear a woman say it in medical school?"

"Well, maybe in medical school."

"Is it so shocking?"

Surprisingly, it wasn't, not when she was the one saying it. "I'm not exactly shocked, but it does make me squirm a little."

"Does it bother you when I say *vagina* or *uterus*?"

"No, but those words come up when you're talking about your work."

"Well the word *penis* comes up in my work too, and I do use it. As you know, I wouldn't *have* any work if it weren't for penises."

She smiled a challenge. Her eyes held his as she tucked hair that had come loose from her ponytail behind her ears.

He gulped back his astonishment and laughed. He'd never experienced a bawdy exchange like this with a woman. It was fun. He laid down a challenge of his own. "You use that word in your work? I kind of doubt that. Give me an example."

She was adorable with her cocky little smile and her face scrunched in concentration. "Oh, I know. I'm looking at a three-month ultrasound with a patient, and I point to the nub below the umbilical cord. I tell the woman, 'That's the little penis.' "

"Yes," he said. "I can see how it would come up in that context. Is that all?"

"No. Let me think. Oh, I know: women ask about how to wash around their babies' penises. They wonder about spots and splotches on their partners' penises. And…"

"Okay, okay you win. I see this is an important word in your vocabulary. And do you use words like that when you talk to your American fiancé?"

"Hmmm. No." She fussed with loose tendrils of hair again, and then, apparently giving up on the ponytail, she pulled off the band that held it and let her hair fall free around her shoulders. "I don't suppose I do. He uses a wide assortment of words to refer to the male reproductive organ himself, but I think he'd be a bit uncomfortable if I started talking about *penises*."

"I'm glad to hear that. It makes me feel less backward."

"Backward?"

He straightened a stack of papers on his desk. "I'm aware that people in your culture are more open than we are about matters related to sexuality. People of my culture must seem quite inhibited to you."

She settled her hair behind her shoulders. Glints of auburn shone from the thick waves. "No, not to me. I don't think *inhibited* is the word I would use. I'd say people of your culture are more *respectful* of sexuality. I imagine more of the mystery and sensuality of sex has been retained."

*Mystery and sensuality.* That brought rather disturbing images to his mind. He saw a seduction scene as she might imagine it, a scene in which his culture was exotic and mysterious. And *sensual*—with incense and brooding music and silken robes—maybe in the desert in a sheik's tent, with rugs and cushions and clusters of grapes.

A dreamy fever clouded her eyes and a fresh bloom crept across her cheeks. Was she imagining that same scene? Was he in it?

Chapter Four

What was wrong with her? Talking about penises and sex. She'd embarrassed him, and now she felt embarrassed herself. He might have thought she was thinking about *him* when she mentioned "mystery and sensuality." She hadn't been, not really. It was just that the temptation to shock him out of his seriousness had been irresistible. And a hint of fire smoldering below his formality evoked those two words. A picture came to her mind of a scene with silk curtains, soft music, and the aroma of heavy incense. *Mystery and sensuality.* The fire in Majid's lush eyes burning into a woman's soul, those competent hands moving slowly over her skin, learning her body. touching and stroking. He had the hands of a surgeon, of an artist. Or a lover.

She shifted in her chair. Where had that come from? She shifted again, and the chair creaked. Her eyes skittered around the room. There was a picture on the wall of a seagull hovering above waves, with wings spread, legs trailing, and body arched. The bird looked very still, held by the wind in a quiet, waiting pose. She looked at Majid. He was watching her, quiet and waiting too.

She thought of Dan. Of Dallas. A memory came unbidden, a detail she hadn't thought of since last spring when it happened: he'd had the idea they could assign numbers to various positions and then he could call them out during sex like a quarterback calls out plays. *Six, four, eight, hike* would mean she was to get on top. They could work out the numbers and the meanings and memorize them.

She'd laughed, dismissing his suggestion as a joke, and he'd laughed too, but she could tell he was disappointed.

She shook her head to clear away the memory. It wasn't fair to compare Dan with a fantasy.

"Are you married?" She expected him to say no. He seemed solitary. He seemed self-sufficient.

"No, I'm not married. But my family is working to change that. I'm being presented with a steady barrage of lovely candidates."

"Oh. Are arranged marriages still common in Behruz?"

"I'd say the country is in transition. Almost everyone in my parents' generation had arranged marriages, and many people still do, but others have courtships like you have in your country and marry for romantic love."

"Where does your family stand on the path of this transition?"

"In the middle, I think. My mom and my aunts and cousins are all on the lookout for suitable women, and I'm willing to meet the ones they recommend, but I won't marry without getting to know the woman first. My parents understand and accept that."

There was such fire and passion in his eyes, yet his plans to find a life partner sounded calculated and staid. "Your way of referring to romantic love sounds pretty cynical," she said.

"Perhaps. Maybe *guarded* is a better word. We've

had a few love matches in my family that had disastrous endings."

Had he been burned himself? That might explain his reserve. "I'm sorry to hear that."

He was solitary, but he wouldn't always be so. He must seem like a good catch to the women his family was finding for him. Layla could imagine the kind of woman he would choose. She would be quietly elegant and beautiful. She would never say the word *penis*.

"I suppose yours was a great love match?" he asked.

"Oh yes."

"How did the two of you meet?"

"It's a romantic story, really. Dan is one of my brother's oldest friends. He spent a lot of time at my house when they were teenagers, and I had a terrible crush on him. They're five years older than I am, so they just saw me as a kid, but then last spring we met again. He saw me as a woman, and I found I still had feelings for him. Nothing had changed. We fell in love practically in an instant."

"Well that does sound like a story right out of one of your Hollywood movies."

Ouch. "You are cynical, aren't you? Actually, it's a story that already played out once in my family with my brother and his wife. They also met as teenagers; she had a crush on him since she was thirteen. They've been married three years now, and you've never seen a couple more in love."

"I see. You're right. I am cynical because of the bad experiences in my family. Your situation is, of course, entirely different. When are you going to be married?"

"In January. When football season is over."

"That's only four months away. Do you have a lot of preparations to make?"

Ugh. Wedding preparations. She hated to be reminded. Her friends and family and even Dan thought she was nuts to make this trip when she had a wedding to plan, but she'd worked like a fury and gotten almost everything done before she came. "Not really. I've done all I can. The last-minute details will be a bit tricky— I'll be moving to Dallas when I get home, and the wedding's going to be in San Francisco—but my mom lives in San Francisco. She'll be a big help."

"Planning a wedding must be exciting."

In fact, planning the wedding had felt like drudgery. She hadn't experienced the dizzy, happy excitement most brides seemed to feel, perhaps because Dan wasn't there to share in the planning. Or, maybe, because she wasn't thrilled about the move. She couldn't really imagine living in *Dallas*, but surely once she got there everything would be okay. Dan loved his new home and was confident she would too. She just had to power through the move and the wedding. Not that she had any choice. She'd quit her job and given notice to terminate her lease, and there was a mountain of towels and linens, all monogrammed with Dan's initials, and a crock pot and a dozen serving dishes and tons more bounty from two wedding showers piled in her living room proclaiming a commitment to her new life.

She suddenly felt that mountain of things was piled on top of *her*. A swell of panic rose in her throat. The dark eyes that regarded her from across the desk made her feel feminine and *appreciated* and, for some reason, confused about the course of her life. She needed to get out of there. "I should be getting back to my uncle's."

"Of course." He moved a pen from one side of his desk to the other. "Please excuse me: I'm afraid I've taken up your whole day."

"Don't apologize. It's not like there's somewhere I need to be. Actually, I was afraid I was holding *you* up." Her hand twitched toward his arm, which lay so near on the desk. What was that? She was *engaged*; she loved Dan. This confusion and strange desire to touch him had to be just nerves and fatigue and reservations about Dallas. Their conversation had become too intimate, which was her fault. What had come over her? Talking about *penises*.

He assured her he was in no hurry at all. He'd finished with his last patient before he went in to deliver Nida's baby.

"Still, it is getting late. I should be going." She stood.

He stood too, and she saw, peeking out from under his slacks, Nike tennis shoes. Nice touch, Dr. Nassiri. Not quite so stiff after all.

She went to the labor room to admire the baby. Nida clutched her hand and said, "I couldn't have done it without you."

Layla smiled. "That's not true, Nida. You did all the work yourself, and you did an amazing job. You're going to be a wonderful mother."

She bent over the bed to kiss Nida on the cheek, then returned to Majid's office. He was seated again, his elbows on the desk, his face buried in his hands. She grabbed her chador and thanked him for dinner. He escorted her to the sidewalk and stood with her while she waited for a taxi.

He thanked her again for her help.

"It was great, and working in the hospital will be too. That kind of thing gives me more connection to the Behruzi culture than life with my family does." She smiled her gratitude.

"I'm glad. I'm lucky you feel that way."

A taxi turned onto the street at the corner. They hailed it, and soon Layla was on her way to the palace.

Back in her room, she used the palace's ancient intercom to order tea from the kitchen. When it came, she settled into the settee in the corner of the room and called Dan. He was in a bad mood. His team had lost a game the previous night because a "jackass umpire" called a fumble when clearly there'd been interference.

After listening for a while to his complaints, she asked, "Do you remember when we first met?"

"Of course. You came with Rashid and his wife to my sister's wedding."

"No. That's when we ran into each other last spring. I mean the *first* time we met. When we were kids."

"No, I can't say that I do."

"It was after football practice for you and soccer practice for Rashid. You gave him a ride home and came into the house with him. I was having a party for my twelfth birthday. Remember?"

"No. Not really."

She sipped her tea. "You stayed for a while to have cake and ice cream."

"Sorry, honey, that was a long time ago. Why do you ask?"

"I don't know. I've been thinking lately about how

it was back then when we were still grieving my father's death and we were trying to adjust to life in a new country."

"Hmmm. I never thought about your family as grieving or as having to get used to anything. As far as I could tell, you were all pretty normal."

"Do you remember the time I went fishing with you and Rashid and you baited my hook?"

"No, not really."

"Or when you and Rashid came to my soccer game?"

"No. Is this some kind of test? You were just a kid, you know."

She said no, it wasn't a test: she was just curious. "I guess you made more of an impression on me than I did on you."

They laughed. Dan told her about the next game.

There was no reason why Dan would remember that birthday party, she thought after they'd hung up. She took a final sip of her tea even though it was now cold.

The birthday party was still clear in her mind…

She'd had two good friends in elementary school: one Behruzi and one Iranian. Layla was the leader of the little threesome because of her fluency in English. She helped her two Farsi-speaking friends make their way in what was a new world for all three of them. They were aware of their "otherness," but it didn't matter because they had each other.

Unfortunately, some quirk of the school zoning system separated Layla from her two friends when they started junior high school. Layla was suddenly on her own in a world of blondes with Anglo Saxon names.

She invited all the girls in her homeroom to the birthday party, and most came, but somehow she didn't feel the party was about *her*. The girls were friendly enough, but they divided into their little cliques, and she felt left out just as she did at lunch every day.

Her mother organized games, and everyone participated, but connections that didn't include her still dominated the scene. Layla found herself laughing too much, competing too hard in the games, wishing she were blonde like Jessica and Ashley, wishing she had an American name, wishing she had *boobs*. She was the only skinny, flat-chested girl in a roomful—apparently a *world full*—of twelve-year-old girls who were already blossoming.

And then Rashid and Dan showed up, and the energy of the party changed. Dan was tall and handsome and *blond*, and actually Rashid was handsome too—although Layla had never noticed it before—and both boys wore shirts that proclaimed their status as high school athletes. The two boys tousled her hair and sat with her while they ate cake and ice cream. Suddenly all the other girls wanted to be with her too. They crowded around, vying for the attention of the high school boys and claiming to be Layla's best friend. Dan and Rashid sang "Happy Birthday" to her, and the other girls joined in even though they'd already sung it when their own cake was served. They sang with more fervor when they sang with the boys, and Layla felt the sense of belonging she craved.

The boys could have left after eating, but they stayed for the rest of the party, showering Layla with attention and making the whole thing more festive and fun.

She had friends after that. The party was the beginning of adjustment to life in America for Layla and the beginning of her crush on Dan.

Somehow it seemed Dan was the magic ingredient that changed everything.

It still seemed like magic—that they'd found each other again when they were both ready for commitment and that the man of her dreams had chosen *her*.

The next evening Layla attended a party at Mina's parents' home in a wealthy neighborhood in the northern part of the city. The party was held in a special room that was apparently reserved for such occasions. There were no furnishings except for large cushions and a long table laden with food, along the wall. Thick Persian carpets in various shades of blue covered the marble floor. The attendees, all women, included Mina's mother, sisters, and aunts, various cousins, and two of Abu-Khan's aunts. Layla, in her long velvet skirt and silk top, was the most informally dressed, but no one seemed to mind

The purpose of the party, besides gossiping and eating, was to watch Mina be decorated with the henna tattoos all Behruzi brides must wear on their hands and feet during their wedding.

Layla was treated as a guest of honor, sitting next to Mina on one of the cushions. She sat cross-legged, eating from a plate of melon and grapes, watching as one of the henna artists worked on Mina's toes. The other guests sat in a circle, watching too and admiring the work. After a few minutes, when the beautiful design was beginning to emerge, a second artist approached Layla. "Are you ready for your tattoos, khanoum?" What Mina hadn't mentioned when she invited Layla was that the guests were going to be ornamented too. Everyone stopped talking while they waited to see if the American visitor would participate.

"Yes please," Layla replied, and she held out her arms. Another cushion was propped against the wall so she could lean back. The artist took her hand and studied it for a moment before beginning the painstaking work. Everyone watched and gave advice and murmured their approval while delicate flowers were painted on Layla's hands, arms, and feet. Layla smiled at Mina and said, "Thank you."

When Layla's tattoos were finished, she stood up and did a pirouette. Everyone exclaimed that she looked beautiful. The artist asked, "Is there anywhere else you'd like a tattoo?"

"Yes," one of the women said. "Your belly." This would apparently be a special added bonus for the American visitor.

Layla lifted her shirt and lowered the waistband of her skirt. She rested back against the cushion while the artist worked. The brush tickled the tender skin of her belly, making her giggle. The other women, who were still gathered around her, giggled too.

Someone suggested Mina should get a belly tattoo also, and Mina agreed. She pulled up her dress, revealing black bikini underpants, and offered her belly for the work. Soon both Layla and Mina had flower petals encircling their belly buttons.

One of Mina's cousins said, "Mina's belly tattoo will probably be gone by the end of the wedding night. The sultan will have rubbed it off!"

Everyone went suddenly quiet. Layla followed their eyes and saw they were watching Mina's mother.

The older woman pursed her lips in disapproval, but her eyes twinkled amusement. Soon a smile overtook her face, and then she laughed. Everyone joined in. The room was filled with laughter, and Layla was filled with a delicious sense of belonging.

Mention of the wedding night reminded Layla that she had to tell the couple about the need for abstinence before the artificial insemination. She hated bringing up such a sober subject, but it had to be done. When everyone's attention shifted to Mina's mother and aunt, who were the next to be decorated, Layla whispered to Mina, "There's something I need to tell you about the insemination." She told her what Majid had said about abstinence. "We're not sure when ovulation will take place, but if you stop having sex three or four days after the wedding, you should be okay."

Mina counted on her fingers. "So that means we can have sex until the last day of our honeymoon?"

"Yes. That should be okay."

"All right. Have you told Abu-Khan?"

"No, but I will."

"Great. Thank you." Mina seemed as comfortable talking about her husband's ejaculation schedule as she was hearing about artificial insemination. It must be only the men of Behruz who were uptight about the subject of sex and reproduction. She could probably talk about penises all day long with the fun-loving women at the party and it wouldn't faze them a bit.

The next morning was Friday, the Moslem day of worship, and also the day of the wedding. Layla dug her mother's gift for Abu-Khan out of her suitcase and went to see if she could find him. As awkward as it might be, she needed to relay the information about the need for a few days abstinence. Hopefully the gift would distract him from her message.

She found Omid in his little office and told him she needed to see the sultan.

"I'm sorry, khanoum, but as you know, the sultan is getting married today." He flashed a broad but insincere, white-toothed smile. "I'm afraid he won't be available until he comes back from his honeymoon. Can I help you?"

"Please, Omid, I need to talk to him. I have a gift. Can you ask? Tell him it will only take a minute."

Omid waited long enough to emphasize his reluctance but finally pressed a button on the intercom. "I'm sorry to interrupt you, Excellency. The young woman seems to think her business with you is urgent." He frowned as he listened to Abu-Khan's reply, and his eyes lanced disapproval when he hung up. "I'm supposed to take you up to his room."

"Great. Thank you."

Muttering about how *no one* was ever invited to the sultan's bedchambers, he led her down the corridor to the palace's lone elevator, which had only two stops, one on the ground floor and the other on the second floor in Abu-Khan's private wing. A guard who stood at attention in front of the elevator pushed a button and the door opened. Layla and Omid rode up together in silence.

Omid led her to Abu-Khan's room and knocked on the door. Abu-Khan's voice boomed, "Enter," and the door was opened by a slender young man wearing a white cotton uniform. Layla followed Omid into a huge room—it was as big as the largest dining room downstairs—that was sumptuously decorated with silk and velvet curtains, massive antique furniture, and exquisite carpets. The smell of perfumed toiletries was so heavy she could barely breathe. Abu-Khan, wearing a velvet robe, lay reclining in what looked like a cross between a throne and a beauty parlor chair. Shaving cream covered the lower half of his face. The young man who'd let them in, Abu-Khan's "groomer" according to Omid, picked up a straight razor and returned to his work.

"I'll be with you in a moment," Abu-Khan said.

Layla and Omid watched the groomer finish his job.

"Shall I do your nails now, Excellency?" the groomer asked.

"I'll talk to the young woman first. You can wait in the hallway." The servant left, but Omid stood waiting.

"You must leave too," Abu-Khan said to Omid.

Omid's eyes shot arrows of accusation at Layla before he turned to join the other man outside the room.

Abu-Khan turned to Layla and spoke impatiently. "Okay, what is this about?"

"First of all, congratulations, Uncle. This must be a very happy day for you. My mother asked me to extend regards from all our family. She sent this small gift." She held out the package, but he motioned for her to place it on a table nearby. It contained, she knew, a photo album with a hand-painted cover embossed in gold.

Layla had asked her mother, "Do you really think he's going to use a photo album?"

Her mother had scowled. "What was I supposed to get him? A toaster oven?"

Abu-Khan waved the back of his hand at her. "You

could have given the gift to Omid. Is there anything else?"

"Yes, uncle. First of all, I need to let you know: I had to tell the doctor the sample I gave him was not from my husband. I couldn't let him continue to think I was the one who wanted to get pregnant."

"But..." Abu-Khan sputtered. He sat up.

"Don't worry. I didn't mention you. I said it was my uncle who needed help. He has no idea I'm related to you."

"Okay, if you're sure..."

"I also wanted to tell you I've spoken to Mina and explained everything. She's happy to cooperate, and she understands the importance of keeping this a secret. She seems eager to demonstrate her loyalty to you."

Abu-Khan tilted his head to the side and smiled. Really, he appeared to have very tender feelings for his young bride. "Good. Is that all then?"

"There's one more thing." She told him about the need for abstinence before the next sample was produced, and she explained when the abstinence should begin.

Abu-Khan's face darkened. He took a deep breath, puffing up his chest. "I will not have my honeymoon period disrupted by the whim of some doctor."

Layla put her hands on her hips. Apparently no one had ever told this arrogant man what to do in his life. "Fine. I'm just relaying the doctor's recommendation. You don't have to do it. It's just a way of *improving* the chances of conception. The artificial insemination could be successful even if you don't abstain, and it could fail even if you do. Remember, there's no guarantee at all that there will be success the first time you try. Even under the best of circumstances it can take several attempts."

"But it must be successful. I want Mina to be pregnant with my heir before you leave. Tell the doctor it's imperative that we have success on the first attempt."

"I'm sure the doctor will do everything in his power to get the result you want. And you... Well, you must do as you wish."

He frowned. He rested back again on his chair. "Tell the groomer to come back in."

She'd been dismissed.

Chapter Five

When Majid arrived at the clinic on Sunday—the first day of the Moslem work week—Saba was already there but Layla wasn't. What if she didn't come? He didn't have her cell phone number, and he had no idea where her uncle lived. She could disappear from his life. She could go back to her nice football coach. She might leave without even telling him.

And then she breezed in, throwing off her chador, greeting him with that smile and her smell of lilac. Her arms and hands were covered with henna tattoos, and she was wearing a T-shirt that proclaimed: *Midwives bring out the kid in you.*

He laughed at the T-shirt. He laughed at himself for his moment of panic. He soaked up her smile and her scent. It had been four days since he'd seen her.

"Are you going to be at the hospital today?" Layla asked.

"No, I'll see that you're settled in with a labor, then I'll come back here."

While Saba found a lab jacket for Layla, Majid asked about the wedding.

Layla put on the jacket. "The wedding? Oh, yes, my uncle's wedding. It was great. Pretty formal and speechy, but still great. Men and women were segregated for most of it, but I guess that's normal."

He laughed. "Yes, that's normal. And being formal

and speechy is too."

She told him and Saba about the tattoo party. "That was the best part," she said. Saba said she'd been to several tattoo parties herself, and she agreed it was the most fun part of a wedding.

Majid looked at Layla's hands, at the white skin visible between the delicate lines of red ink. He thrust his own hands into his pockets, resisting the urge to touch her. The tattoos might give him an excuse to do so. He could lift one of her hands and hold it while he studied the designs. He could comment, in a kind of impersonal way, on the beauty of the work. He might trace the lines with his fingers. It would all seem normal in her culture, wouldn't it?

But it wouldn't be normal in his. He couldn't do it. Especially not with Saba watching.

He said, "I hope the scrubbing you'll be doing today doesn't destroy the beautiful artwork."

"Oh well, I'll still have tattoos on my feet. And in one other place." She smiled an I-have-a-secret smile. "I'm not going to mention where."

Saba laughed. "I can imagine where."

*Oh great*, Majid thought. Now *he* would be "imagining where" for the rest of the day.

****

It was after eight when Layla kissed her second labor patient on the cheek and went to find Majid. She'd called him after the baby was born and told him she'd be done in about half an hour.

She found him waiting at the nurse's desk outside the maternity ward.

"You look exhausted," he said. "You should have left sooner."

"Yes, I know. I thought about it, but I just couldn't leave the woman."

"Well, I know you made a huge difference—for the women you helped in labor and for the staff who saw or heard about what you did. Thank you."

As they walked through crowded spaces filled with shabby benches toward the front door of the hospital, she thought about what she'd seen in the maternity ward. Not enough staff. Not enough equipment. Not enough space. Not enough honoring of the sacred nature of birth.

She understood even better now the importance of Majid's doula project. She wished she could help more.

But she was leaving Behruz in less than three weeks. To move to Dallas.

\*\*\*\*

Majid led her to his car near the emergency entrance and opened the door for her. He should never have roped her into this. She was exhausted.

"I'm sorry, but I can't take off just yet. One of the orderlies is bringing some supplies I need in the clinic." They were in the front seat, leaning back against the headrests. Her eyes were closed. "I can never thank you enough."

"It was great. I'm the one who should thank you."

Her hand rested on the seat between them. He reminded himself he would never have the right to touch it. And then in the next moment, without his volition, he reached out and took it. She didn't open her eyes. Her hand was soft; it relaxed into his. He wanted to caress it; he wanted to hold it against his face. But this had to be a casual touch, a just-interested-in-the-tattoo touch.

"The henna held up very well," he said.

She smiled her keeping-a-secret smile, still resting back against the headrest, still with her eyes closed. "I wasn't worried about it. Even if it got washed off my hands, it would still be on my feet and in that *other place*."

"I've been imagining all day long where that *other place* might be. You are going to tell me, aren't you?" He rested his hand, still grasping hers, on the seat between them. He was acting like an adolescent, but he couldn't help it. He wasn't just *acting* like an adolescent; he felt like one.

Her smile broadened. "No. I like that no one knows it's there."

He watched her. He held her hand and watched her and thought of all the places on her body where a henna tattoo might be hiding.

He held her hand until he saw the orderly coming across the parking lot toward them.

When the supplies had been loaded, Majid suggested they go to a restaurant, but Layla said she didn't feel like being out in public. "Is the street vendor still working at your clinic?"

"I think we can catch him if we hurry." Majid started the engine.

When they got to the clinic, he introduced Layla to Mohammed.

She said, "Majid considers you to be the best chef in the city, and I have to agree with him."

The old man grinned his pleasure while he served their kebabs and rice.

They ate at Majid's desk again. They were alone in the clinic, alone in the dark night.

"Your effort today was successful beyond my fondest hopes," he told her.

"Oh good. I kind of forgot my reason for being there once I got involved."

"I can imagine you did. I heard the nurses talking about your work when I was waiting for you. They said your first patient would have had a cesarean if you hadn't helped her."

"That was the plan when I got there. They were waiting for an operating room to become available. Her blood pressure was high, but she was just scared, and she was having back labor. Once she felt supported and had relief from the back pain, her blood pressure normalized."

A truck rattled past the clinic. In the distance a siren wailed. Inside the office, all was silent except for their quiet voices. "I heard you have an interesting trick that relieves back labor."

"Yes, I do. Actually, there are lots of things the patient can do to relieve back pain, but most of them involve getting out of bed. I didn't feel like tackling that issue today, but in the long run, if you have trained doulas working in the hospital, you'll have to loosen up on that."

"I know labor patients need to move around, but some of our doctors are opposed to the idea."

"Yes, I met one of them. A Dr. Mansur. I don't think he approved when he saw my patient on her hands and knees on the bed. I can just imagine how he'd have reacted if I had her doing lunges in the middle of the ward."

Majid smiled and sighed. He swiped a piece of bread across the last traces of meat and spices on his plate. "So you met Dr. Mansur. I told you about him. He's the head of the department, and he's the doctor most resistant to the idea of having doulas in the labor ward."

"What else can I do to help?"

Majid dropped the empty plates into the wastebasket. "I'd like you to do what you did today once more if you have the time. I want as many of the doctors and nurses as possible to witness—or at least hear about—the value of labor support.

She thought for a moment. "Yes. I can do it once more this week."

"How about the day after tomorrow?"

"That will be fine."

He offered to give her a ride home, but she declined. "My uncle wouldn't want you to know where he lives."

"This is ridiculous, Layla. I'm a doctor. Even if I did figure out who your uncle is, I would never tell anyone about his medical problems. Can't you explain that to him?"

She laughed. "You'd have to meet him to understand. He's *very* paranoid about this."

"All right.

He asked for her cell phone number. "I may need it later, after the insemination when there are lab results."

That was lame, but she didn't seem to notice. She picked up a scrap of paper from his desk and wrote the number.

He waited with her for a taxi and helped her into it when one appeared. He watched it drive away, taking her back to the uptight uncle who was, thank God, an uncle and not a husband. He took the piece of paper from his pocket and memorized the number she'd written. Then he scolded himself. She wasn't a patient and she wasn't married, but she was an American, she was engaged, *and she was leaving soon.*

\*\*\*\*

Layla spent the next day in the neighborhood where she'd lived as a child. She went to see Rashid's old friend Reza in his pharmacy.

"Salaam, khanoum," Reza said.

She pulled off her chador. "Hello Reza. I'm Layla, Rashid's little sister. Do you remember me?"

He came out from behind the counter and took both her hands in his. "Layla," he said. "Little Layla all grown up. You are a beauty, my dear." He gave her almond candies of the kind he'd given her when she was little. "See, I do remember."

She remembered too.

She gave him a gift from Olivia, a framed picture of Olivia and Rashid and their four-year-old son Jamie. Reza wiped tears from his eyes as he studied the photo. "I helped them escape."

"Yes, I know. Olivia told me."

After saying goodbye to Reza, she walked down not-quite-forgotten streets inhaling not-quite-forgotten smells: raw meat hanging in the butcher shops, meat and spices cooking in the homes, camel dung, garbage, kerosene, and exotic flowers. She said salaam to everyone she met. The child she'd been when this place was home sang in her heart.

Standing in front of the gate of the house where she lived for the first seven years of her life stirred old memories. Children squealed with laughter behind the wall of the house next door. She'd been a child like them, here, in this country, in this neighborhood. She'd played in a courtyard like theirs, behind walls like theirs, feeling safe and protected. She'd had a father then, but her memories of him were vague now.

Women wearing chadors had led her around the city. She'd expected to grow up to be like them, but she hadn't; she didn't need to hide. She removed her chador and folded it over her arm as she walked past a shop that sold produce and another that sold kitchen supplies. Her mother would have shopped in these stores or in ones like them. She felt comfortable with the curious glances she received. Her roots had been nurtured in this soil, but her branches had blossomed in California sunshine. Well, California sunshine and San Francisco fog. The two cultures blended in her, in her blood and in her heart. Had she thought the blending was a weakness? Now it felt like a strength.

Two children, a boy about six and a girl about three, peeked at her through the iron bars of a gate. She smiled at them; she said salaam. They ran from the gate toward their house, giggling. The boy called "Salaam" as he disappeared inside.

She thought about Majid as she walked. He might be treating a small child's injury—she pictured him bent over the imagined child with that kind, attentive doctor expression on his face—or maybe he was delivering a baby. She reached into her pocket now and then to wrap her hand around her cell phone, hoping to feel the vibration of his call.

But no call came.

The next morning she got up early and called on the intercom to have her breakfast of flatbread, cheese, and strawberry jam sent up to her room. She dressed while waiting for the food to arrive, thinking of Majid as she selected a T-shirt, even though she might not see him today. She remembered his expression when he read the words on the T-shirt she wore last time. As he *looked at her breasts* and read the words. He blushed and smiled, looked away and then looked again. And then he laughed, an open, hearty laugh, and she laughed too.

She went directly to the hospital this time. There were two patients in the labor ward: one who was flying through labor with her fifth baby, and a seventeen-year-old named Chista who was just starting active labor with her first.

Layla sat between the two women and encouraged them both. After the older woman's baby was born at ten-thirty, she spent the rest of the day helping Chista. Two other patients arrived during the afternoon, but Chista needed all her attention.

The baby was born at seven.

Layla left at seven-thirty, expecting to go out to the street for a taxi. But Majid was sitting in a little waiting area outside the labor ward.

Still high from the last birth but tired too, she felt an urge to throw herself into his arms. Only the starchy nurses watching and Abu-Khan's warning about touching men stopped her.

"How long have you been waiting?" she asked.

"Not long. I had the nurses call when the baby was born; I left the clinic then."

"Oh. I see." The feeling of wanting his arms around her grew stronger. His shoulder beckoned. Her eyes were drawn to a flat area just below his collar bone. Her cheek would rest nicely there against the soft fabric of his suit jacket.

He asked where she wanted to eat, and she said "somewhere quiet." He said, "Okay, I know the perfect place." He took her to a restaurant in a small hotel on the northern edge of the city where the land began its slope up to the mountains. The hotel was surrounded by gardens filled with flowering shrubs and dahlias. A waterfall splashed through a ravine cut into a foothill behind the hotel. The city lay spread out below, its lights twinkling in the hush of early dusk.

"What's this placed called?"

"The hotel is Hotel Abshar, which means *hotel by the waterfall*. The mountain, Mount Rustam, is named after a legendary hero of Iranian and Behruzi folklore."

"What a beautiful setting."

"How did it go today?" he asked when they were seated beside a window that looked out over the city.

"I had a delivery with Dr. Rahbar."

"Yes, so I heard."

"He was going to cut an episiotomy, but I talked him into waiting, and the baby was born without one."

Dr. Rahbar had been routinely cutting episiotomies for forty years, and he'd never shown any interest in current research on the subject. Yet Layla had convinced him to wait. Layla with her henna tattoos, her thick lashes, her lilac scent, and her ridiculous shirts.

Was she wearing one of those shirts today? His eyes drifted down—from her flashing eyes to her chest, to her small, firm breasts, which were outlined under the shirt. To the words stretched across those breasts: *Trust birth.*

He relaxed. He'd been tense all day, worrying

about her, wondering how it was going for her, feeling like a heel for throwing her into an environment that might disdain her direct, non-medical ways of assisting birth.

"Where do you get these shirts?" he asked.

She looked down to see which one she was wearing and smiled. "My patients give them to me."

"Oh, of course." Women probably showered her with gifts to show their gratitude after she delivered their babies.

The waiter took their orders and disappeared into the kitchen. Layla said, "I showed Dr. Mansur a little trick that speeds things up when the baby is having a hard time getting past the pubic bone."

"I heard about that. The nurses were talking about it. What do you do?"

"It's something the patient does, actually. It's called a 'pelvic tilt'. Do you know what that is?"

He shook his head.

"Of course not. Why would you? Yoga instructors teach it, and some childbirth instructors do too. The woman just tilts up her pelvis, lifting the tailbone and shifting the pubic bone out of the way. It often helps, especially if the woman has to lie on her back while pushing."

*Just tilt up the pelvis.* Amazing. The simplicity of the solution left him in awe. *Her* simplicity—and her directness and her dedication—left him in awe.

"Was Dr. Mansur impressed?" he asked.

"I doubt it. He didn't give any indication that he was." Layla laughed. "Maybe a little."

"Well the nurses were."

Their food was served. While they ate, they talked

about labor and about reforms needed in the hospital. She told him about her upbringing as a half-Behruzi but really mostly American girl in San Francisco. He told her he also had a Christian mother.

"Really? Is she American?"

"No." He smiled that indulgent doctor smile of his. "She's Armenian, born and raised in Behruz. There are Armenian Christians all over the Middle East: over 150,000 in Iran and about 60,000 in Behruz."

"Oh. I didn't know that. How did your parents reconcile their religious differences? What were you taught?"

"In this country the father is responsible for the religious education of the children. In my case, the main teacher was my grandfather: my father's father. We lived in his compound with various aunts and uncles, and he held formal classes for me and my cousins. It was all very regimented and strict."

She thought being "regimented and strict" would have suited Majid just fine. "Did you mind?"

"No, not at all. I was in awe of my grandfather. I considered it a privilege to spend time with him. I think my greatest fear when I was a child was that I wouldn't have an answer when he called on me in class. And my greatest pleasure was earning his approval. He used to pat me on the head and call me his 'little scholar.' He was my strongest supporter when I wanted to go to the U.S. to study medicine."

"Is he still alive?"

"Yes, but my grandmother died two years ago."

Layla dipped the tip of her finger into the melted wax of a candle that flickered in the middle of the table. She could picture Majid as an avid student at his grandfather's knee. "Did your mother have any say in your religious upbringing?"

Majid gazed out over the city. "I was an only child. She and I were alone together a lot. She used to pray with me, and she told me Bible stories, so I guess I learned both traditions at the same time. They kind of melded in me. Their basic principles felt the same."

Layla hadn't thought she'd ever find anyone outside her own family who felt that way. "It was the same for me. We started going to church when we went back to the States, but my mom took us to a mosque too and kept up many of the Muslim traditions in our home. I grew up feeling that the two religions were talking about the same thing. What about your family? Did they know your mother was exposing you to Christian ideas?"

"Yes, although they may not have known the extent of it. They didn't object. Everyone loves my mother, and they respect piety no matter what the religion."

"So they wouldn't have minded if you'd come back from the States with an American wife?"

He laughed. "Oh that they would have minded very much. My grandfather's greatest fear was that I would do exactly that."

"I remember you mentioned there's a history there…"

"Yes. One of my uncles married an American when he was in college in Florida. He brought her here when he graduated, but she never adjusted. She went back to the States after about a year, taking their baby son and leaving my uncle devastated. Eight years later, just about exactly the same thing happened with one of my older cousins—except at least that time there wasn't a baby involved. So everyone in my family thinks American women are shallow heartbreakers. My grandfather made me promise before I left that I wouldn't get involved with an American woman."

It was hard to believe he'd managed *that*. "You must have been gone almost ten years if you went to college and medical school. Do you mean to tell me you didn't have any involvements during all that time?"

He chuckled sheepishly. "Let's just say I managed to return home with my heart still intact, which I believe was my grandfather's primary aim."

His heart intact. What an image. Intact, not given to another, not broken. Beating strong in his breast, ready for love. The image of his strong, *intact*, beating heart was visceral. His shoulder, that place where she would put her head if she were to press her body against his, still beckoned.

Strange disquiet churned in her. She glanced at her watch. It was almost ten. They'd talked for nearly two hours.

He checked his watch too. "Oh I'm sorry. I had no idea it was so late. I know what a long day it's been for you."

The lights of the city were blinking off one by one. Only two other tables were still occupied in the restaurant.

"Thank you for dinner," she said.

"Thank you for the work you did today," he said.

"I'll let you know when my uncle's wife is ready for the insemination. Call me if there's anything else I can do."

Majid hesitated. "I'm not sure I should impose on

you any further, but there is something…"

"Yes?"

He looked at his watch again though only a few minutes had passed since the last time he checked. "It's late, and this will take some explaining. Can you come to the clinic tomorrow? Maybe at lunchtime? I'll tell you about it then."

Abu-Khan and Mina would be returning from their honeymoon tomorrow. She might not be able to just saunter away from the palace whenever she wanted to once they were back.

But she was intrigued. And she wanted to see Majid again. She said, "Sure, that will be fine."

She called Dan when she got back to the palace. "I just wanted to say I love you," she said.

"It's great to hear from you, but I can't really talk right now. I'm leaving for work."

"Okay." Disappointment sliced through her. She needed to reconnect with him. She said again, "I love you."

What she meant was, *Please love me too. Please love the part of me that needs to be here. Say something that will remind me of all we share, something that will break the spell that this place—and a certain complex doctor—are casting on me.*

He said, "I love you too, kiddo. Gotta go. Talk to you later."

Chapter Six

Majid watched Layla study the Arabic script of the menu. She'd taken off her chador as soon as they sat down, revealing the word stretched across her chest, *Vagenius*. He looked around to see if any of the other diners might understand the word, but they were all Behruzis and no one was paying attention to them. He smiled at her audacity.

Her hands moved slowly over the foreign words as she tried to decipher the offerings on the menu. Her fingers were long, slender, and *delicate*. Like her. The patterns of the henna tattoo were fading but still visible.

She looked up from her effort. "This is a lot like the Chinese restaurants back home, except for the fact that I can't quite read the menu."

He helped her translate the choices from Farsi to English. He ordered Mongolian beef, and she ordered sesame chicken.

"I remember the first time I went to a Chinese restaurant in Minneapolis," he said. "It reminded me of this place. It seemed strange that a Chinese restaurant would be the thing to trigger nostalgia for Behruz."

He talked about his life in Minnesota: how hard it was at first—adjusting to the harsh winter, studying and writing papers in a second language, navigating a new culture. He joined a club for students from the Middle East, but he found he had little in common with students from countries like Turkey, Saudi Arabia and Iraq. At least he shared a common language with the Iranians and Afghanis, and he did meet a few other Behruzis. By the end of the first semester he was making friends with Americans he met in his classes.

And he found his dark eyes were attractive to American women.

"Of course." Layla laughed. "Those shameless, shallow women who left your heart intact in spite of their best efforts."

"Yes, those."

Blood rose to his face as he remembered those days. He'd felt guilty when he found himself attracted to women he was forbidden by his family to love, and yet the unaccustomed freedom and the more relaxed attitude toward sex made them irresistible. His grandfather definitely would not have approved of his behavior. He didn't approve of it himself.

Layla talked about her family: about her younger sister, Suzi, still single, her older sister, Salma, who was married and had four children, and her brother, Rashid, who was expecting his second child with his wife Olivia. While Layla and Suzi had gone to college in Oregon, the older two had attended UCLA.

"So that explains the UCLA T-shirt you were wearing the first time I met you."

"Yes. It was a gift from my brother." A waiter served their food, and Layla scooped a bite with her chopsticks. "You remember what I was wearing?"

"Yes, Layla, I remember what you were wearing. You made quite an impression on me that day—with your American clothes, your ponytail, and your little jar of semen." And with her beauty, her earnestness, and her surprising candor.

She blushed. "And don't forget my unsupportive husband."

"I'm not about to forget him. I couldn't forgive him for abandoning you to take care of everything yourself."

"I was pretty unhappy with him too when I saw him through your eyes. If he hadn't been, you know, *imaginary*, I might have considered divorcing him."

Majid told her about the project he had in mind. Before he applied to the American foundation for a grant, he had to get approval from the Behruzi Health Department. He wanted her to help prepare the proposal. Could she do the research and maybe help him think through some of the details? He wanted data about similar projects in other developing countries. How much money was saved? How many fewer cesareans were there? How many fewer deaths? What type of woman would be suited for the job of doula? How would they recruit them? What would the training entail? How would the doulas' work be scheduled?

They brainstormed each concern in an energetic discussion that had them concentrating, arguing, laughing, and gesturing with their chopsticks. They finished eating and the waiter cleared the table, but still they talked on. Majid had never had anyone to talk about the project with before. He thought there would be more support for it now that some of the doctors had seen Layla in action. Hopefully.

Layla's eyes were alight with enthusiasm and her face was glowing. "I'd love to help, but I'm only going to be here two more weeks."

"Yes, I know." *Sixteen more days.* He'd been

counting. "It doesn't matter. Do as much as you can with any spare time you have." He asked her what she needed for her research.

"Just access to a computer," she said.

She could use the one in his office. He scribbled the various passwords she would need on a paper napkin. He asked when she could start.

"Today," she said. "I'm free this afternoon."

She was free. Like a butterfly. She was all grace as she pulled her chador over her head and as they stepped out into the sunlit world. She might fly. She might flap the edges of her chador like wings and take off. Her essence was that light and free.

They walked from the restaurant back to the clinic together, still brainstorming, still laughing, still gesticulating. Her face glowed—from the fresh air and sunshine and from her passion about the subject.

When they reached the clinic, he found his aunt Soraya sitting in the waiting room, wearing her dark chador.

Soraya raised herself stiffly from the chair. She stared at Layla, who had thrown off her chador as soon as she entered the building: at her pink cheeks, carefree smile, and flashing eyes. At her long, coltish legs, her arms covered in henna tattoos, and the word *vagenious* emblazoned on her shirt. Thank goodness Soraya couldn't decipher that word.

"Aunt Soraya," he said, "how nice to see you. What brings you to the clinic? I hope you're not ill."

Soraya tore her eyes from Layla to glare sternly at Majid. "I just came by to pick up some paperwork for Nessa." She looked pointedly at Layla and then back again at Majid, waiting for an introduction. And an explanation, of course.

"This is my aunt Soraya," Majid said to Layla. "Her daughter Nessa is my bookkeeper."

Layla's smile had faded. Her posture and eyes were alert, sensing danger.

Soraya's eyes beamed accusations at Majid. Saba sat at her desk watching it all, a smile crinkling the corners of her eyes but her lips pursed tight.

"This is Layla Shirvani, Aunt. She's from America."

There was an inquisitor's challenge in Soraya's voice as the two women went through the ritual greetings.

Soraya asked Majid. "What has brought her to our country?"

"She came to Behruz for a wedding, and now she's staying for a short time to visit with her relatives here. She's helping me with a project."

"I see…" Her scowl said she didn't like what she saw.

There was an awkward silence while Soraya waited for explanations Majid wasn't inclined to give.

"It's time for me to get started on my work," Layla said in her breezy way. "It was nice to meet you, khanoum." To Majid she added. "I'll be at the computer."

She disappeared down the hallway that led to his office.

When she was gone, Soraya turned her inquisitor's eyes on Majid. "What's going on here, young man?"

Soraya and various other aunts had been like second mothers to him when he was a child, when they all lived in his grandfather's compound. It was no surprise that she thought she had a right to interrogate him or that his mind went automatically into defensive mode. *Nothing's going on. She's just helping with a project. Our relationship is strictly professional. She's only been here a few weeks. I barely know her. She's engaged. She'll be gone soon.*

But he didn't want to explain Layla's presence in his life. It would confirm Soraya's assumption that she had a right to judge his relationships. For once in his life he felt the choices he was making were none of his family's business. He was thirty-one years old—an educated man and respected doctor—and yet his family still seemed to think he needed their approval for everything he did.

He shouldn't have allowed that to go on this long.

He said simply, "Layla is a colleague, Aunt."

Then he turned to Saba, who was staring at him wide-eyed, having heard the entire exchange. "Saba, would you see if you can find the information my aunt needs? Thank you." To Soraya he said, "It was, as always, lovely to see you, Aunt, but please excuse me. I have to get back to work."

His first afternoon patient was arriving, limping badly and with a face contorted by pain. Majid helped the old man with the door and said kindly, "Good afternoon, Agha Bashir. I see your gout is acting up again. You can come right back to the examining room."

Soraya pursed her lips and shook her head. His mother would probably hear about this meeting tonight when the family came together for their weekly dinner at his grandfather's home. He couldn't take the time to mollify Soraya. He gave her a quick kiss on the cheek and then offered Agha Bashir his arm and led him to the examining room.

When he passed the open door of his office, he saw Layla gazing intently into the computer screen with a pen poised over a pad of paper. She glanced up and smiled her carefree smile. A hint of her lilac scent wafted into the hallway. He breathed it in while continuing down the hallway, mentally preparing for the next thing he would smell: the pungent aroma of the old man's sweaty, swollen foot.

\*\*\*\*

Layla ate with Abu-Khan and Mina that evening. They were like teenagers in love, tittering at private jokes and giving each other flirtatious looks.

Abu-Khan sobered when the after-dinner melon was served. He twiddled his fork, banging it against his water glass, which rang a clear, musical tone each time it was struck. He cleared his throat. "So what's the first step in this baby thing?"

*Baby thing*? How many times did she have to explain this? "I'll go to the pharmacy for the predictor kit tomorrow morning, and then we can begin watching for ovulation."

Abu-Khan's fork clanged against his plate. "Kit? What kind of kit? What are you going to do?"

Layla sighed, and Mina giggled her happy, newlywed giggle. "Don't worry," Layla said to Abu-Khan. "You won't be involved at this point. In a few days, you'll have to produce a sample like you did before, and then you'll do it once more the following day. The kit I'm going to buy will help us figure out the best time to start the process."

He set down the fork. "You aren't going to hurt

Mina, are you?"

Mina and Layla grinned at each other. Really, his devotion was so out of character it was funny. "No, nothing we're going to do will hurt." She asked if they'd remembered about the need for abstinence.

Layla and Abu-Khan both lowered their heads like children who'd been chastised. Mina smiled mischievously.

Good grief. "All right. But if you could control yourselves starting now until after the insemination, it might help."

"Yes, of course," Mina said, all diligence and compliance. "Do you have money for the kit?"

Abu-Khan might be helpless when it came to the practicalities of daily life, but apparently his new wife wasn't.

"Actually, I might not have enough. I still haven't had a chance to change money. And we'll need cash when we go to the lab too. They'll charge extra if we end up asking them to do the sperm washing on the weekend."

Abu-Khan seemed irritated with such details, but Mina teased and coaxed him and insisted that he take care of it.

It was eight-thirty when Layla returned to her room. She read for an hour and then called Dan. He was eating breakfast.

"Hi, kiddo, how are you?" She hadn't liked that nickname when she was an adolescent, and she found she liked it even less now. Not that she liked *darlin'* any better. Before she could answer, he started telling her about the previous night's football game.

She said "yes" and "mmm-hmm" and "wow," now

and then, trying to show an interest, but really the fact that his team had won was all she needed to hear. She loved the enthusiasm and happiness in his voice, but the details of the game went over her head.

"I better get going. I have to analyze the video of the game before practice. I love you. I can't wait to see you."

Why hadn't she ever told him she didn't like the nickname kiddo?

She called her mother and told her about her dinner with the newlyweds. "They really seem to be in love."

Mary laughed. "Will wonders never cease?"

And Layla talked about her work with Majid.

Her mother appreciated the importance of what Layla was doing. She said, "And to think I thought you'd be bored if you spent a whole month in Behruz."

Layla thought about her mother's remark as she got ready for bed. She'd never been less bored in her life. She was eager to start another day of research. Another day in Majid's clinic. With Majid stopping in now and then to see how she was doing. Stopping in, leaning over her shoulder to see what she'd found online, his cheek just inches from hers, his enthusiasm spurring her on to find ever more evidence of the value of his project. His project that was beginning to feel like *their* project.

Chapter Seven

Majid was, as usual, the last to arrive at his grandfather's home for the family's regular weekly dinner. Female voices hushed when he entered the salon where everyone gathered before the meal. There were speculations in the women's eyes. And questions and accusations.

Apparently Aunt Soraya had spread the news to his other aunts and his female cousins. He wasn't surprised; he'd known it wouldn't take long. The men would eventually be told, but not until the women gathered more evidence and had time to evaluate the situation.

He kissed his mother's cheek, ignoring the questions in her eyes, and smiled at Soraya, who beamed triumphant in her role as the one to "break the story." He didn't feel as intimidated by the disapproval of these women as he had in the past. He would try to reassure his mother, but he wouldn't offer explanations and justifications, not even to her.

He joined the men at the other end of the room, kissing the hands of his father and grandfather and bending over to let them kiss his forehead. They motioned for him to sit between them on the soft, embroidered velvet of the largest sofa in the room. Grandfather asked about his work, but of course he only wanted to hear it was "going well." He wasn't interested in the problems of old men with gout or young women having babies.

They talked about the search for oil in southern Behruz, which had seemed promising at first but was now being acknowledged as a failure. Majid's father bemoaned the loss of hoped-for wealth for the country, but Grandfather thought it was a good thing. He said, "At least, as a poor country with no oil and no access to the sea, we're left in peace by other countries." Conversation moved to the sultan's recent appointment of a new ambassador to France, which both men approved. Like most of the middle and upper classes, they loved their ruler.

Majid barely listened. His mind was full of the information Layla had assembled that afternoon. She'd found references to half a dozen doula projects like the one he wanted to implement in Behruz, and there was plenty of good evidence showing they reduce costs, save lives, and benefit new mothers. He remembered how Layla's eyes flashed with enthusiasm as she talked. Those expressive, candid eyes were beginning to haunt him.

After dinner his mother joined him. She hugged him to her ample bosom and then led him to a settee in a corner of the large salon. "Is there something you need to tell me, Son?"

"I'm not getting involved with the American woman Aunt Soraya saw in my office today—if that's what you want to know."

Love and concern glistened in her eyes. "All right, dear, if you're sure…"

"She's helping me with a project. Really. That's all."

Doubt furrowed her brow. "Just be careful."

If he kept talking about Layla, his mother would see her concern was well founded. Better to change the subject. "You never told me about my birth, Mother. How was your labor?"

Her face relaxed. "I don't think anyone has ever asked about that." She smiled a rueful, remembering smile. "Most women had their babies at home in those days. Your father's parents wanted me to have you with their doctor here in their home—we were living here then—but I wanted to be in my own parents' home with the midwife who'd delivered my aunts' babies and my sisters' babies. We reached a compromise. I had you in my parents' home with the midwife, but the doctor checked in now and then and was there at the end in case there was a problem. Everything was normal, so he stayed out of the way during the delivery."

"Who was with you?"

"Let me see… The midwife and my mother, of course, and two of my older sisters—your Aunt Navideh and your Aunt Alma."

"Was Father there?"

She laughed. "Oh no. He was in the next room, but I could feel his nearness and his love the whole time."

"It sounds like my birth is a happy memory for you."

She grasped his hand. "Oh yes. It was the most memorable day of my life. It was painful, but it was beautiful too. And it brought me you."

"Well Mother, you may not know this, or you may not have thought about it, but almost all women in Behruz today are alone during labor. They have no family members with them. A few lucky ones get a little support from a kind nurse, but our hospitals are so understaffed that the nurses can't really afford to spare more than a few moments. Can you imagine what it's like to go through that experience alone, in a cold hospital ward, afraid, and without any emotional support at all?"

"Oh dear, I never thought about that. No one ever talks about it."

"I don't think many of today's women have positive experiences like you did."

"Really? None of your cousins has ever said a word about what went on during their time in the hospital. We see them pregnant, and then we see them with their new babies. It's like the time in between didn't really happen. It's a blank."

"I think it's a blank for them too. They feel somehow that their fear and despair and their inability to deal with the pain are their fault. They feel they've failed as women. They can't bear to recall it."

"This is heartbreaking to contemplate. Why are you telling me?"

"Because I want to change the situation. I want to start a program that will train non-medical women to support women in labor. The American woman is helping me apply for a grant. She's a highly trained midwife, and she's passionate about labor support."

"Oh, dear Son, I'm very proud of you." She wiped away a tear.

"I think of you, Mother, when I imagine the women who will be providing support. I want kind, nurturing women like you."

She squeezed his hand and smiled, but then concern crossed her face again. "How long will this

American woman be staying in Behruz?"

"Just two more weeks."

"That's probably for the best, dear. I can tell you admire her very much."

It probably *was* for the best. He and his mother stood and embraced. Then he took his leave of his father and grandfather and returned to his apartment a few blocks away.

He thought about his mother's words, *be careful*. His mother only knew one of the reasons why caution was advised. Layla was *an American*. He knew the other reason. She was engaged to an American Adonis.

He opened his billfold and pulled out the little scrap of paper that bore Layla's cell phone number. Not that he needed to see it written: he still remembered it.

He pulled out his own cell phone and dialed the number, but then he stopped. What would he say? He'd be seeing her tomorrow. She'd said she was coming in tomorrow, hadn't she? Or had he just assumed it? Suddenly he wasn't sure. Maybe he should check.

\*\*\*\*

Layla was in bed reading when her cell phone rang.

The deep voice that answered her "hello" was familiar. Just the one word, *salaam*, was enough. Her heart started a happy dance.

"Hello, Majid." She dropped her Kindle and nestled down deeper into the plush linens.

"Are you busy?"

She laughed. "No. I'm in bed, reading."

"I'm trying to picture that."

She sighed and stretched. "I'm in a huge canopy bed under the softest comforter ever made, wearing an old flannel nightgown—sorry, it's not sexy at all—

and…" She stopped herself. She was doing it again, veering into inappropriate territory. But this time it was partly his fault, saying he was "trying to picture that."

"And what?"

"And I'm smiling."

"Because?"

"Because I'm happy you called."

He cleared his throat. "Well, that paints quite a picture. Thank you."

She grinned at her own nerve. Really this man brought out something very impudent in her. "What about you? Where are you?"

"I'm on the sofa in my living room, my feet stretched out on the coffee table, shoes off, a cup of hot tea beside me, and…"

"Yes?"

"Smiling."

"Because?"

"Because you are."

That made her smile even more. "The scene you just described should include a cat curled up in your lap and a fire burning in the fireplace."

"Sorry, no cat, no fireplace."

He asked if she was going to the clinic the next day, and she said she was. He told her he'd never had a pet, and she told him about her tomcat Sam who slept at her feet for most of her childhood. They talked about the weather in San Francisco, the weather in Minnesota, and the forecast for the next day in Behruz City (high of 31 degrees Celsius, low of 17). They challenged each other to translate from Celsius to Fahrenheit in their heads, and Layla won, calculating that the high the next day would be 88 degrees Fahrenheit and the low would be 62.

After they hung up, she hugged a spare pillow and pictured Majid, stretched out with a cup of tea in his hand, until she fell asleep.

The next morning Omid handed her a package wrapped in tissue paper and secured with tape. It would be the money for the ovulation kit. Omid scowled at the package and at her. Poor guy: he seemed to hate not being "in the know" about everything that went on in Abu-Khan's life.

Layla took a taxi to the pharmacy Majid had told her about. Even with her face mostly hidden by her chador, asking for the kit triggered a discomfort she wouldn't have felt back home. Speculation glinted in the eyes of the clerk, a skinny young man with thick glasses, but only for a second. He answered in a neutral, professional voice and quickly produced the kit.

Back in the palace, she asked Omid to tell Mina she wanted to see her.

"Do you have an appointment with the sultana?" Omid asked.

Really. She wasn't asking for access to the crown jewels. "No, I don't exactly have an appointment, but I believe she's expecting me."

"What should I tell her is your reason for wanting to see her?"

Layla understood Omid had to screen requests to see Abu-Khan and Mina, but still... Everything she was doing was *at Abu-Khan's request*. "Just ask her if she can see me, please."

Omid punched some numbers on the intercom and had a brief exchange with Mina. When he finished, he said in begrudging tones, "The sultana will see you in the sultan's bedchambers. I will escort you."

"That's okay," Layla answered cheerfully, as if she heard nothing but cordiality in Omid's voice. "I remember the way. Just let the guard at the elevator know I'm coming, please."

Ha. Omid was no doubt hoping to hear some clue about her business with the royal couple.

As she started down the long hallway that led to the elevator, Abu-Khan, wearing a business suit, came striding toward her from the other end, flanked by two men who were dressed as he was. Two palace guards followed the more officious-looking men.

Abu-Khan was speaking and his two associates were leaning toward him, listening with rapt attention as they walked. Layla prepared to say a nice formal and obsequious salaam and started sifting through the various terms of respect she'd heard others use, terms like *Excellency* and *Glorious Leader* and *Exalted One*, thinking she should use one of them, but Abu-Khan either didn't see or chose to ignore her. In fact, it appeared she was invisible to all the men in the group. She moved to the side and hugged the wall to avoid being trampled as the little group streamed past.

Okay. Now she had a better understanding of her role in the palace.

She and Mina sat in comfortable chairs at the far end of the room where she'd watched Abu-Khan be groomed on the morning of his wedding. The door to the bedchamber was open, showing walls covered by silk tapestries, mirrors in gilded frames, and a canopy bed even larger than the one in her room.

She explained the test and then waited while Mina peed on one of the strips. When Mina came back from the bathroom, she showed the strip to Layla.

"It'll take a few minutes," Layla said. She reminded Mina that it wasn't likely there'd been a surge yet. "Based on what we know of your cycle, I would expect the surge to occur the day after tomorrow." The two women waited, their hands clasped, staring at the wet strip. Time ticked slowly by.

After about five minutes Layla said, "Okay, no surge yet. We'll check again tonight and then every morning and evening until it comes."

Mina asked "When it's time for the insemination, will you be the one to perform the procedure?"

She'd been assuming Majid would do it. "I'll check with Dr. Nassiri, but I don't think he'll mind."

Layla stood, but still Mina clung to her hand. "Please, I want it to be you."

"I'll ask him when I see him later today."

Layla went right to work at the computer when she got to Majid's clinic. He passed by the open door of the office a few minutes later and paused to say good morning. When his glance fell to the words on her shirt and lingered there for a moment, Layla glanced down to see which shirt she'd worn.

*Don't ovary act.*

Maybe this one was too silly.

Three hours later, they sat at Majid's desk eating a lunch prepared by Mohammed.

"How's it going?" Majid asked.

She told him she was finding so many studies that confirmed the value of doula support it was only a matter of selecting which ones to cite.

"What specific benefits do they mention?" he asked.

"Nothing that would surprise you." She told him about a book by respected French obstetricians that summarized the results of several studies. The book concluded that the use of doula support reduced the overall cesarean rate by 50% and the length of labor by 25%. They also reported fewer incidences of maternal fever, a reduction in the number of days newborns spent in infant care units, fewer babies born with symptoms of infection, higher rates of breastfeeding, decreased rates of postpartum depression, and greater confidence observed in the new mothers' handling of their babies. "Doula programs have been initiated in Guatemala, South Africa, Japan, Mexico, and all over the world, really. The results are so consistent and so widely known, I don't think you have to demonstrate the value of doula support in your grant application."

"You're right," he said. "The grant committee in the U.S. should be an easy sell. They actually *want* to give money to projects like ours. It's the Behruzi Health Department I'm worried about. The material we present to them has to emphasize cost savings."

"No problem. There are studies that show that too. I'll have something written up in a couple of days."

"Great. Really, I can't thank you enough for doing this."

His appreciation sent shivers tingling up her spine. What a rare man he was to be devoted to a cause most men would find hard to understand.

She asked if it would be all right for her to be the one to inseminate Mina. "I've inserted hundreds of IUD's. This won't be much different from that."

Neither of them had ever performed an intra-uterine insemination, but it was a simple procedure they both felt confident to perform. Majid said, "Technically you shouldn't practice medicine in Behruz without being certified, but there's no real enforcement of the rule. Since your aunt knows you, and I'm sure she'd prefer a woman anyway, it makes sense for you to be the one to do it."

They'd both found in their reading that opinions varied as to the best timing. They compared notes and decided on a plan that would involve two inseminations twenty-four hours apart.

"It's likely the surge will occur on the weekend. Will the lab be open?"

"I already asked about that. The technician has agreed to come in especially for this if he needs to. For a price, of course. That won't be a problem, will it?"

Layla stifled a laugh. If he only knew. Abu-Khan was probably the richest man in Behruz. "No, that won't be a problem."

Majid gave her two sterile jars, his cell number, and the address of the lab. He assured her he'd assembled what they needed for the insemination.

They were ready.

"How was your dinner last night?" she asked. "Had your aunt spread the word that a frivolous, immoral American woman has infiltrated your world?"

His rueful smile answered the question. "Yes. And there is wide concern about the safety of my heart under such a threat."

"I hope you were able to reassure them."

"I had surprisingly little interest in reassuring them. I did try to put my mother's mind at rest, and she understood the nature of our collaboration, but, as for the rest of them, I guess they need something to gossip and cluck about. It might as well be me."

*And me*, Layla thought. Oh well. Let them view her as some kind of Jezebel. It wasn't likely she'd ever see Soraya again or meet any of the rest of them.

Wrong. Just as she was having that thought, two chadored women about the age of Aunt Soraya appeared at the door of Majid's office.

Majid sighed a longsuffering sigh. He stood up. "Salaam Aunt Jalileh. Salaam Aunt Bibi. To what do I owe the great pleasure of having a visit from you today?"

Layla saw the scene through the eyes of the two women: the remains of lunch spread all over Majid's desk, her ponytail—darn, she should have worn her hair down—her jeans and the T-shirt. What did the T-shirt say again? Oh, yes. *Don't ovary act*. Too bad they couldn't read the English script. Overreacting was almost certainly on the agenda.

Both women had let their chadors fall loose around their shoulders, revealing their tailored dresses and high-heeled shoes. With their careful makeup, lacquered hair, and manicured nails, they must see her as a total bumpkin. Or as a total *American*, which was apparently even worse.

Majid repeated his question and one of the women replied, "Since we were in the neighborhood shopping, we thought we'd stop by to say hello."

"How very kind of you," Majid replied with a civility that sounded sarcastic to Layla but probably sounded normal in this culture that placed so much value on formal exchanges. He introduced Layla, and she stood too.

"I'm pleased to meet you." She extended her hand.

Aunt Bibi squeezed it and smiled shyly, but Aunt Jalileh buried her hands under the folds of her chador and scowled.

"You're an American?" Bibi asked.

"Yes. That is, my mother is American and I live in the States. My father was Behruzi."

"Oh, you're half Behruzi," Bibi said, smiling, nodding, and muttering "*bali, bali, bali*"—yes, yes, yes—as if Layla's half-Behruziness were a tremendous achievement. "When will you be returning to your home?"

"In less than two weeks," Layla replied. *And then I'm getting married to my American fiancé, so you have nothing to worry about.* She didn't say the words that would reassure them. If Majid didn't want to explain, then she wouldn't either.

Saba buzzed to tell Majid his first afternoon patient had arrived.

"I'm sorry, but Layla and I have to get back to work."

The aunts hesitated, giving Majid a chance to explain what Layla's work might be, but he was busy clearing away the debris from their lunch.

Layla sat down and waited while Majid nudged his two aunts out of the room. Bibi looked back over her shoulder with that same shy smile. "It was nice to meet you."

Layla returned the smile and the sentiment and went back to work.

Hmmm. Being snubbed by Jalileh hadn't triggered her usual need to ingratiate herself. Hmmm indeed.

\*\*\*\*

Majid took several deep breaths, trying to calm the

irritation caused by his aunts' visit. It had been unpardonably rude of Jalileh to refuse the handshake. He needed to apologize to Layla. Not that she'd seemed upset. He hoped there would be no more *spontaneous visits* by other aunts. Maybe once Aunt Jalileh and Aunt Bibi reported their findings to the women of the family, interest would wane. Since those findings included the fact that Layla was leaving soon, the women might be satisfied that the family was safe from the evil intentions of another conniving American woman. He could only hope.

Layla wasn't in any way conniving. He knew that. She was the most direct and ingenuous woman he'd ever met. Yet there was something about her that didn't add up. What was it? Her talk about the Adonis back home made him sound more like a beloved celebrity than a boyfriend. Majid hadn't heard anything that made him think her soul was *nurtured* by the man.

Still, she was engaged. Majid had to accept that. It seemed American women could make commitments without really knowing their own hearts—and those commitments often turned out to be as shallow as the fickle hearts that made them.

He wanted to shake her. He wanted to wake her up.

Majid did know his own heart, and he could see it really was in danger of exactly what his aunts feared for him. He needed to shake *himself* and stay alert to the risk of caring too much for this bewitching, *American* woman.

Chapter Eight

Layla ate dinner with the newlyweds again. "You can do the ovulation test yourself tonight, can't you?" she asked Mina.

"Oh, no," Mina cried as if she'd been asked to deliver her own baby. "You have to help me."

Abu-Khan glared at Layla in his imperious I'm-the-sultan way. "Of course you will help her."

Ignoring Abu-Khan, Layla spoke directly to Mina. "I have no doubt you could do it yourself, but I'll be glad to sit with you. I know how nerve-wracking it can be to wait."

Mina's smiled her relief. "Thank you."

"Since I'll be visiting you twice a day for the tests, would you mind arranging for me to come and go without having to be escorted by Omid?"

Abu-Khan sputtered something about "palace protocol," but Mina interrupted him. "Of course."

That evening Layla set out for the royal chambers without bothering to consult with Omid. The guard greeted her with a cheerful salaam and opened the elevator door. *Take that, Omid.*

Abu-Khan sat on a velvet couch in a corner of the room watching America's Funniest Home Videos dubbed in Farsi while she and Mina repeated the ritual with the ovulation strip and learned that the hormone surge had not yet occurred. She gave Mina the two sterile jars to keep until they were needed.

Mina joined Abu-Khan, who was chuckling at a montage of cats chasing dogs, while Layla slipped through the door and returned to her room.

She called Dan.

"I've been thinking," he said, "none of my friends in Dallas can come to San Francisco for the wedding. We should have a reception here."

"Oh. In Dallas?"

"Yes, darlin'. Here. In the city where we're going to make our life together."

"When were you thinking of doing that?"

"As soon as possible after the wedding. Right after we get back from our honeymoon."

Layla wouldn't know a single person at that party. "All right; that will be nice. Will you be able to do some of the planning before I get there?"

"No, I'm not good at that sort of thing, but I was talking to a friend of mine, Brittany—she's the cheerleading coach—and she said she'd help. She knows all the services in Dallas: caterers, florists, music groups, and stuff like that."

A caterer, a florist, and live music. This was beginning to sound like another wedding.

"Okay… I'll start thinking about that."

Great. I can't wait. I want to invite the other coaches and their wives and the whole team with their girlfriends. It's going to be a blast.

Layla agreed that it would be a wonderful party, but after she hung up she felt overwhelmed. Now she had to plan a reception while moving and getting ready for her wedding and finding a new job.

The next day, while working at Majid's computer,

she looked up to find an older woman with her chador draped over her arm standing in the doorway. Another aunt? This one was a grandmotherly sort of woman, with soft, well-padded contours and graying dark hair pulled back into a bun. She was wearing a knee-length straight skirt and a matching jacket.

"Hello. You must be the American who's been helping my son," the woman said.

"Yes. I'm Layla. You're Majid's mother?"

"I am. My name is Zora."

"I'm afraid Majid isn't here. He had to go to the hospital to perform an emergency appendectomy. Can I help you? Would you like to wait for him?"

"I would if you don't mind. Majid told me about you and the project the two of you are working on. I was hoping to meet you."

"How nice. Have a seat." She arched her back and stretched her shoulders. "I could use a break."

Zora took the seat across the desk from her.

Saba came in with two steaming cups of tea, and they thanked her. While they sipped the hot brew, Layla told Zora about a study she'd found that morning that described a doula project for poor women in Bombay.

"Majid told me about conditions for laboring women in the general hospital. What you're doing is going to make a big difference."

The warmth of the woman's voice was genuine. Of course. She was Majid's mother. She was the kind of woman who would raise a sensitive man like Majid.

"I've met a few of your sisters," Layla ventured.

"You did? I know you met Soraya. She's my sister-in-law, not my sister. Who else have you met?"

Layla thought for a moment. "I believe their names

were Jalileh and Bibi."

"Oh really? They are wives of my husband's brothers. When did you meet them?"

"They came by yesterday when they *happened* to be in the neighborhood."

Zora's eyebrows lifted. "Oh dear. I hope they weren't rude. They don't have a very good opinion of American women."

Layla smiled. "I could tell. Jalileh was a *little* rude, but I didn't take it personally."

Saba burst into the room. "A patient has just come in, khanoum. She's in really hard labor. What should I do?"

Layla jumped up from the chair. "Call Majid, call the nurse, and get me the woman's chart."

She found the laboring woman in the waiting room, bent over one of the chairs breathing through a strong contraction.

The woman's husband stood beside her wringing his hands. "I tried to get here sooner," he explained. "I had to wait for my brother to come with the car, and then there was terrible traffic on Karush Street."

When the contraction ended, Layla helped the patient walk back to the labor room. "Could you come too?" she asked Zora. "You might be able to help."

The husband followed, still wringing his hands and still explaining why he hadn't gotten his wife to the clinic sooner.

She found a clean gown in one of the drawers and handed it to Zora. "Could you help her get into this and help her get onto the examining table, please?" Zora did as she asked, speaking in a quiet, gentle voice to the patient and pausing during each contraction. Layla washed her hands and donned a paper gown. The husband huddled miserably in a chair in the corner of the room.

Saba brought the woman's chart and told Layla, "Doctor Nassiri says you are to deliver the baby if he doesn't get here in time." As if Layla had to be told. What else was she going to do?

Layla glanced at the chart to find the woman's name. "Don't worry, Darya. Everything's going to be fine. Dr. Nassiri is on his way, but I can deliver your baby if he doesn't arrive in time. I'm a midwife. I've delivered over a thousand babies." She looked at the chart again. "I see this is your third pregnancy and your other labors were fast. It looks like this may be another fast one. Do you mind if I check you?"

The young woman nodded, and Layla proceeded with the exam. "Just as I thought, Darya, you're getting close to delivery. I know your contractions are intense. Relax as much as you can, and breathe through them like you did with that last one. You're doing beautifully."

Saba stood anxiously at the door. "Is there a delivery tray ready?" Layla asked.

"Yes, khanoum Layla. The nurse always prepares one before she leaves after a birth."

"Could you get it for me?"

"Oh yes, of course."

Layla motioned for Zora to stand on one side of the laboring woman and for her husband to stand on the other side. "Talk to her," she said to both of them. "Encourage her."

The husband was mute, but Zora knew what to say. She wiped the woman's brow with her handkerchief.

"You're doing beautifully, dear child. Your baby will soon be in your arms." Zora looked unsurely at Layla, who nodded and mouthed the word *perfect*. Zora's soft, motherly voice continued its encouraging words.

Saba brought the delivery tray and placed it on a table beside Layla.

Darya's face scrunched in effort.

"Wait, don't push yet," Layla said. "Let me check you again."

She checked and told Darya it would be fine for her to push if she felt like it. The young woman's eyes grew round with fear.

"You're doing so well, Darya. It won't be long now. Can we help you get into a squat?"

It was too late for a change of position. Another contraction began and Darya's face scrunched into a pushing grimace. Layla had Zora and the husband each take one of Darya's hands.

"That was a great push," she told Darya. "Just a couple more like that and you'll be holding your baby."

Five minutes later, Darya *was* holding the baby, a beautiful little girl with a thick mop of dark hair plastered wet against her scalp. Darya's husband had relaxed, melted really, and was bent over the baby examining tiny fingers and toes. Layla checked while she waited for the placenta to be born and reported that Darya hadn't torn. Zora was beaming like a new grandmother.

"You were wonderful," Layla said to Zora. "Thank you."

There were tears in the older woman's smiling eyes. "No, thank *you*."

\*\*\*\*

Warmth swelled Majid's chest as he listened to the two women discuss the birth they'd just witnessed. They sat across from him at his desk: on the left, his beloved mother; on the right, wearing a T-shirt that proclaimed *Midwifery is a work of heart*, the beautiful, smart, irritating, funny, irreverent American woman who had charged into his life with a jar of semen in her delicate hand.

"You were a great help," Layla said to Zora.

His mother smiled. "I don't know about that, but I must say it was a moving and amazing experience."

The nurse had arrived and was taking care of Darya and the baby. Zora said she had to get back home to prepare lunch. "Can I have a peek at the baby before I go?"

"Yes, of course," Layla said.

All three stood. Zora kissed Majid on the cheek and then turned to Layla with warmth and respect in her eyes. The two women liked each other. Majid hadn't realized how much it mattered to him that they did. They embraced, and then Zora went into the labor room.

"Thank you," he said to Layla. Words of admiration and feelings he had no right to express clogged his throat. He held them back. *Thank you.*

\*\*\*\*

"Okay, tomorrow's the big day," Layla told Mina and Abu-Khan that evening when the ovulation predictor strip showed the hormone surge they'd been waiting to see. Even though Mina must have been ovulating every month for years, she and Abu-Khan beamed at each other as if it were a great achievement.

Abu-Khan turned to Layla. "What does this mean?

Do I have to produce a sample tomorrow?"

"Yes." She reviewed the entire process one more time.

"Do you have the bottle and everything?" he asked.

"Yes, Mina has two bottles."

"All right then." The grave expression on his face suggested that masturbation, an act he no doubt performed regularly, was suddenly a responsibility greater than running a country.

Layla explained again the importance of getting the sample to the lab quickly after it was produced. They all agreed to meet in Abu-Khan's chambers the next morning at nine-thirty. She said goodnight and prepared to leave.

Abu-Khan asked her to wait.

"You can go along to bed," he said to Mina. "I have a few more questions for Layla."

Mina accepted her dismissal cheerfully. She said goodnight to Layla and disappeared into the bedchamber. Abu-Khan led Layla to a pair of stuffed chairs in the corner of the room where they could sit facing each other. He raked his fingers through his hair and drummed his fingers on the arm of the chair.

What was this about?

He answered her unspoken question. "It's about Olivia."

"Olivia?"

"Yes. I want her to forgive me for...well, you know, for that business with her son. Could you call and ask if she'll consider it?"

"By 'that business' do you mean your interference in her relationship with Rashid and your trying to claim their son as your own?"

"Um…" He looked around the room and started to stand, but then he sighed and settled back into the chair. "Yes, that."

"I'm sorry, Abu-Khan, but if you want Olivia to forgive you, you have to ask her yourself. Why is it suddenly important?"

His fingers made more trails through the lacquered mass of his hair. "Because of Mina. Because I really have a chance of having a baby now. I'm afraid Allah won't let it happen." He sobbed one explosive, plaintive cry, and then turned away to compose himself. "I'm afraid I'll be denied the honor of having a son if she doesn't forgive me."

"Please don't forget, Abu-Khan: if Mina does conceive, the baby may be a girl."

"I know that. And you know what? I don't even care. I want a son—I *need* a son—but now I know that what I really want is a *child*. With Mina. If Allah will be so benevolent as to give me a child, even if it's only a girl, I'll love that child. Tell Olivia I'm sorry. I didn't know what having a baby meant. When she was pregnant and when she was caring for Jamal, I was so preoccupied. Karen was dying, and a rebellion was brewing. I just didn't see. But now that I have hope of having my own child—with Mina—I understand what it means."

"I repeat, Abu-Khan, you have to ask Olivia yourself. Do you have her phone number?"

"Could you just find out if there's any hope at all? Could you ask her to consider the possibility? I'm begging you."

"All right. But if she does agree to consider it, you'll have to talk to her yourself."

He grabbed her hand. "Thank you. Tell her I didn't understand. Tell her what an angel Mina is. Mina shouldn't be punished for my sins."

What a contradictory man Abu-Khan was. "Yes, I'll tell her."

Back in her room, she placed the call. She told Olivia what Abu-Khan wanted and why. She told her that Mina was, indeed, a very sweet girl.

"I don't see how I can forgive him, Layla. I'm sorry."

"Don't apologize to me, Olivia. I'm not saying you *should* be able to forgive him. I wouldn't if I were you. I'm just passing along his request."

"Thank you for understanding."

"So you want me to tell him no?"

"Not yet. I'd like to think about it for a few days."

"Okay, take your time. You're a saint for even considering it."

They talked about Olivia's pregnancy, and Layla assured Olivia she was still planning to be there to deliver the baby. She would fly to San Francisco two weeks before the due date and stay until the baby came—no matter how long it took.

She didn't display any doubt while she was talking to Olivia, but afterward she worried that her return to San Francisco so soon after getting to Dallas—while she was supposed to be planning a reception—would add stress to her relationship with Dan. She'd mentioned to him, more than once, that she was planning to deliver Olivia's baby, but now she wasn't sure he'd been listening. Would he remember when the baby was due? Had she really explained that it might mean spending as much as three weeks in San

Francisco?

She needed to remind Dan now, but the thought of doing it aroused such dread. He might see her commitment to Olivia as another defection. He already thought she was being selfish by spending so much time in Behruz when he needed her in Dallas, and she could see his point.

She had to tell him.

She could call him now. It was nine in the morning in Dallas—he might be still home—but she was exhausted, and the conversation was going to be agonizing.

She'd do it tomorrow.

Instead she called Majid.

****

Majid had just finished cleaning up his dinner dishes and was making a cup of tea when his cell phone rang. He looked at the caller ID. Layla. Her sweet, soft voice answered his "salaam."

He took his cup of tea into the living room and sat on the sofa, his legs stretched out on the coffee table. "I was just thinking about you. I mean I was thinking about the birth today, about how fortunate it was that you were there to cover for me. My indebtedness to you is growing so fast I can hardly keep track of it."

That it had been a "work of heart" for her resonated in her words. "I was happy to help. I miss delivering babies."

"Of course. You must be anxious to get home and back to work."

She sighed "I don't have a job in Dallas yet, but I don't think I'll be delivering babies. Dan wants me to find work in administration or teaching, something with a regular schedule. You know—so we can have a normal life."

"Oh yes." Of course the blond Adonis would want Layla at his side every possible moment. What man wouldn't? But still, to ask her to give up the work she loved… He was as ready to condemn the man for that as he had been when he thought he wasn't supporting Layla in her desire to become pregnant.

"I do like teaching. And there might be some kind of job in administration I'd like. Or in a clinic—working with pre- and postnatal patients but not delivering babies."

There was resignation in her voice. She was trying to talk herself into the prospect.

"How's the ovulation watch coming?" he asked to change the subject.

Her voice brightened. "That's why I called. We have a surge. Tomorrow's the day."

"That's great. I have the cell phone number of the technician who's going to prepare the sperm. I'll call him now to tell him we'll be doing the procedure tomorrow. What time should I say you'll be coming in?"

"I told my uncle and his wife we'd get started at nine-thirty. We should be on our way to the lab by ten."

"Is your uncle going with you?"

"No. He's still afraid someone might think less of him if they knew he had a fertility problem. He's even asked me and his wife to hide ourselves behind chadors while we're at the lab. She'll be covering her face when we get to your clinic too."

"Don't worry. It won't be the first time—not for the lab and not for me. Are your aunt and uncle

111

excited?"

"I'll say. At least my aunt is. My uncle is a bit unnerved. He wants a baby as badly as she does, but it's disconcerting for him to depend on a process that's so outside his control. And bewildering. He has only the most rudimentary understanding of the anatomy of reproduction. Don't you teach sex education in this country?"

Majid laughed. "You mean in the schools? Are you kidding? No, we are not talking about sex in the public schools."

"Well, I don't think my uncle went to public schools, but whatever his education was, apparently it didn't include the slightest hint of anything to do with reproduction. This whole process has him quite stupefied."

"It will be interesting to see how he reacts when there's an actual pregnancy."

"Yes. I hope I get to see that before I leave."

Right. She was leaving in fourteen days.

He was still counting.

## Chapter Nine

"Okay, just relax right here for about half an hour," Layla said to Mina after she'd finished injecting the sperm. She adjusted the sheet that covered Mina below the waist while Mina adjusted the chador that covered most of her face.

"Thank you, Layla. Thank you, Dr. Nassiri," Mina said, her voice choking with emotion.

Layla squeezed Mina's hand. Majid bent over Mina to make himself visible through the peephole she had in the folds of cloth. "*Inshallah* one of those little swimmers and your egg will meet and fall in love and join together to make you a beautiful baby."

"Inshallah," Mina repeated. *God willing.*

Layla said it too. Inshallah. It was the most gentle way to remind Mina that the outcome was in no way guaranteed.

The next day they repeated the process. Abu-Khan produced another little puddle of royal sperm, they got it "washed," and Layla injected it into its new home.

Inshallah, they all said again.

That evening at dinner, Abu-Khan whispered to Layla, "Have you spoken to Olivia?"

"Not yet, Abu-Khan. If I don't hear from her in a few days, I'll call again."

An hour later, when Layla had returned to her room, Olivia did call.

"It's the strangest thing," Olivia said, "but the more I think about what Abu-Khan wants, the more I feel—I don't know—just kind of *light* about the idea of letting go of my resentment. The fact that he knows what he did was wrong means a lot to me."

"Are you telling me that you *are* willing to forgive him?"

"I guess I am. I'm not saying what he did was okay or that I'd want to invite him to dinner, but I'm tired of having bitterness and blame in my heart. I think I need to let go of it before my baby is born. It would be a gift to myself. My life is so full. I have Rashid and Jamal, and soon I'll have our little girl. If Mina can be happy with Abu-Khan—if they can make each other happy— then I don't want to stand in their way. Tell Abu-Khan I release him. If the word is important to him, tell him I *forgive* him."

Tears pricked Layla's eyes. "It would be much better if you told him yourself, Olivia."

"Yes, I know." Olivia sighed. "Okay, tell him to call me. If he can manage to squeeze out a sincere apology, I think I can put his mind at rest."

Wow. Tears slid down Layla's cheeks as she fathomed the depth of her sister-in-law's goodness and generosity. Rashid was lucky to have Olivia in his life. Layla was too.

Majid was with a patient when Layla arrived at the clinic the next day. They didn't have a chance to talk all morning, but just when the first pangs of hunger struck, she looked up from the computer to find him standing in the doorway, watching her and smiling. He had a stethoscope draped around his neck.

"Are you ready for lunch?" he asked.

She arched her back and slanted her head from side to side to stretch her neck muscles. He was staring at her shirt, at her breasts, or at the words written across her breasts. Which shirt was she wearing today? She glanced down and read, *Yes, I Deliver.*

She cleared away the papers she'd been working on and stood. "Yes. I'm starving."

"How's your aunt doing?" Majid asked when lunches they'd purchased from Mohammed were spread out on the desk.

"About as well as most women in her situation. We have eleven more days to wait before we can test for pregnancy, and she's a little nuts already. I spend at least half an hour with her each morning, and then another half hour in the evening trying to help her relax. She'd love to have me stay with her all day, and my uncle has tried to pressure me into doing that, but I had to draw a line. I suggested she spend a few hours each day with her mother, and he agreed to that. It seems to be helping."

"I sympathize. The wait must be agonizing."

"I just hope this attempt is successful. I can't imagine her having to go through this again, maybe several times, without me here to help keep her sane."

He cleared his throat and seemed about to speak, but then he shifted in his chair and said nothing. She asked, "Is there something else?"

He laughed. "You read me well. Yes, there is something…" He cleared his throat again and slid his chair closer to the desk. "My mother wants me to invite you to our family dinner tomorrow, but I'm not sure it's a good idea."

"Oh, really? I'd love to see your mother again.

Why wouldn't it be a good idea?"

"It's our regular weekly dinner at my grandfather's home. All my aunts, uncles, and cousins on my father's side will be there. I've told you about their attitude toward American women and you've met three of my aunts, so you have an idea what to expect."

"Oh, I see. Yes, the prospect is a bit daunting." She grinned at him. "But I'd love to have an experience of typical Behruzi family life. And I'm not one to back away from a challenge."

He chuckled. "I'm not sure how 'typical' my family is, but if you like a challenge, this could be the event for you. My mother really wants you to come."

"Could you ask her to watch out for me—in case I need protection from hostile aunties?"

"I'm sure she's already thought of that. And I'll be there too, equally willing to run interference."

"Great. Tell her I'd love to come."

His lips quirked in a smile that was doubtful but also amused. "All right. I hope you don't regret it."

The next morning Layla was awakened by a buzz on the intercom. Omid, who appeared to have grudgingly resigned himself to her role in the royal couple's life, said the sultana wanted urgently to see her. She dressed quickly and hurried to the royal chambers, fearing the worst—that Mina might be bleeding.

Mina was waiting for her, sitting on a settee near the door, wringing her hands. Abu-Khan stood at the far end of the room, fingering his prayer beads.

"I'm not pregnant," Mina wailed. She held something out for Layla to see. A soggy home pregnancy test strip.

"Oh, Mina, sweetheart." Layla sat beside the younger woman. "It's too early for a pregnancy test. I told you that. You have to wait eight more days. This means nothing."

Mina sniffled. "Really? You're not just saying that?"

"Really. Where did you even get a home pregnancy test?"

"My cousin bought it for me."

"What?" Abu-Khan strode toward them. "You weren't supposed to tell anyone."

Layla's stern gaze stopped him in his tracks. "Abu-Khan, this is a stressful time for Mina. She needs to be able to confide in someone. If she is pregnant, it will be a normal thing to have happened." She addressed what she knew was really worrying him. "There's no reason why anyone will question how it came about."

Mina said, "I didn't say anything about what Layla did to help. I just said I was hoping I was pregnant. My cousin won't tell anyone."

Layla put her arm around Mina's shoulders. "Don't worry, Mina. It's normal to want to talk about it. Whether you turn out to be pregnant or not, all the feelings you're having are normal, even your eagerness to confirm the pregnancy when it's still too soon." She frowned at Abu-Khan but continued her soft tones as she spoke to Mina. "You just have to be patient a little longer."

The two women stood and embraced.

Still with her arms around the younger woman, Layla said to Abu-Khan, "I spoke to Olivia. She wants you to call her."

"What?" Alarm and hope warred on his face.

"What did she say?"

"You have to speak to her yourself, Abu-Khan. Here…" She released Mina and handed Abu-Khan a piece of paper with Olivia's phone number on it. "You can call now—it's evening there—or you can call tonight after eight."

Mina disappeared into the bedroom, apparently sensing that this was a subject that didn't include her.

Abu-Khan's fingers attacked his neatly combed and lacquered hair. "Do you know what she's going to say?"

Layla sighed. "I think if you demonstrate that you truly regret what you did, she'll say something that will reassure you. Not that you deserve it. She's an amazingly kindhearted woman."

\*\*\*\*

Majid scanned the salon as he'd done a hundred times that evening, in search of Layla, and once again he found her engaged in a cheerful conversation with one of his relatives. This time it was his cousin Jala, who was eight months pregnant. His mother was with them. Layla was beautiful in a long, flowing dress that was modest in every detail but somehow managed to look incredibly sexy. Her hair hung to her shoulders, wavy, thick and shining. All he could think about was twining his fingers through it.

His eyes were drawn to the place on her chest where he would normally find some outrageous word or slogan, but what he saw now was…breasts. The soft fabric that covered them wasn't tight, but still he could make out their shape. Small. Firm. Perfect.

A tap on the shoulder made him turn around, and when he did, he discovered Aunt Soraya scowling up at him. "I see you've invited your American friend tonight. Don't you think you should have checked with your grandfather before bringing a stranger into a gathering that is normally reserved for family?"

He gave her the smile he used when dealing with his most difficult patients. "Hello, Aunt Soraya. Actually it was my mother who invited Layla. I'm sure she did check with Grandfather first."

"Your mother? Really? Why would she do such a thing?"

His smile didn't waver. "I believe it was out of a desire to show hospitality to a foreign visitor in our country."

Soraya made a clicking sound with her teeth and shook her head—a gesture approximately equivalent to a *harrumph* in English—and went over to talk to Aunt Jalileh. She would be eager to share the news that it was *his mother* who invited the infidel into the fold.

Layla, his mother, and Jala had disappeared while he was talking to his aunt. He found Jala's sister, Naji, and asked, "Have you seen Layla or Jala?"

"I think they went to one of the bedrooms. Jala was talking about some kind of pain that makes it hard for her to walk, and Layla said she knew of an exercise that might help."

Of course. He headed down the corridor toward the bedrooms. When he heard feminine voices talking and laughing behind one of the doors, he knocked. "It's Majid. Can I come in?"

His mother opened the door. Jala was on her hands and knees in the middle of the room. Layla was kneeling beside her, her hand on the small of Jala's back. Both women glanced at Majid and then returned

119

to their work.

Layla was coaching Jala. "Sway your back again…and now arch it again. Good. Now sway and arch once more. Great. And now swing your hips from side to side like you're dancing the hula. That's it. Good."

When they'd gone through the sequence two more times, Layla said, "Okay, stand up and see how you feel. Take it easy; go slowly. Majid, maybe you could give her a hand?"

Majid helped his cousin to stand, and then they all watched while Jala took a turn around the room. "It's gone." she said, grinning. "The pain is completely gone."

"Great," Layla said. "The baby must have been pushing uncomfortably against the pelvis. Maybe he was pressing on a nerve. Your movements have helped him shift into a better position, but he may shift back. If he does, just do the exercises again and you should be okay."

"Thank you, Layla." Jala gave Layla an exuberant hug. "I've got to tell Gaspar what happened." She left to find her husband.

"Well, well, well…" Majid said. "I think you've won over at least one member of the family."

Layla's lilac scent and the heat of her smile flooded him like a drug. "Your family isn't as unfriendly as you think," she said.

Good. Apparently they'd been on their best behavior. He exchanged a knowing look with his mother. She knew how the family, especially the elders, felt about American women.

Later, back in the salon, Jala said she wanted to

introduce Layla to another cousin, Rachel, who was three months pregnant. Majid and his mother watched the two young women walk across the room.

"She's lovely," his mother said. "I can see how much you care for her."

"Oh Mother, it's not what you think. She's returning to the U.S. in a week." His voice cracked. "She's engaged. To a *blond American* in Texas."

"Oh dear. I was so afraid for you, and now the worst has happened. I'm sorry. You should have told me. I wouldn't have invited her. American women really are all the same, aren't they?"

"No Mother, she's not like Uncle Hamlik's wife and cousin Ghobad's wife. She hasn't promised me anything. I've known from the beginning that she's engaged and that she'd be going back to the U.S."

Aunt Soraya came up to them. "I forgot to mention, Majid, I want to invite you to have dinner with us Monday. My friend's daughter Elmira will be there. You remember her, don't you?" She continued on without waiting for an answer. "Anyway, she remembers you, and she's looking forward to seeing you again." She winked at Majid's mother.

Majid took a deep breath before answering. "Salaam, Auntie. Thank you for thinking of me, but I couldn't possibly come next week. I'm working every available moment or a proposal for a project at the hospital."

"Oh I see…" She directed a suggestive lift of the eyebrows at Zora.

His mother ignored Soraya and her matchmaking efforts. "Tell me, dear, how is your grant application coming along?"

Soraya made that clucking sound with her tongue and went to talk to her sister-in-law Jalileh.

Majid told his mother that he and Layla had been working each day after the last clinic appointment to hammer out the details of the budget for the doula program.

He didn't tell her they'd been eating dinner together each evening and talking and laughing together and planning and hoping together.

He didn't tell her he was falling in love with Layla.

The concern in his mother's eyes said she'd guessed. He choked back his love and hope and the guilt he felt about having feelings for a woman who was engaged to another man.

He hadn't touched her—well, except for her hand—and he wouldn't. He hadn't spoken his feelings. And he wouldn't. He would spend every minute with her he could, and then he would let her go back to her blond American fiancé and her real life. No one but his mother would ever guess what it cost him to say goodbye.

Chapter Ten

The next afternoon, Zora appeared at the open door of Majid's office.

Layla stood. "Salaam, Zora. I hope you are well. Majid's with a patient."

"Actually, I wanted to talk to you," Zora said.

"Oh how nice. Have a seat. Would you like a cup of tea?"

The older woman declined the tea and sat down. "Thank you, my dear. There's something I want to ask you. It's a bit delicate."

Was this about Zora's health? Or another pregnant cousin? Or was it something personal, something to do with her relationship with Majid? She wasn't ready to discuss *that*. "What is it, Zora?"

"I need some medical advice. It's not for me. It's for one of my sisters-in-law—I'm not supposed to tell you which one."

"Yes?"

"She's my age, or a little younger, about fifty I'd say, and she's having trouble when she is…um…*together with* her husband. She says the experience has become painful. She wondered if you knew of an exercise or medicine that would help."

Layla considered for a moment. Zora might be asking for herself, of course. Layla gave her a reassuring smile. "Did she say if it's a matter of too little lubrication? Does she feel dry?"

The older woman blushed. "I don't know. She didn't say. She just said it hurt."

"It's probably dryness. That's common at her age. I do know of a medicine that would help—it's an estrogen cream—but I don't know if it's available in Behruz, and even if it is, I wouldn't be able to prescribe it. Majid—or any other doctor—could, but they'd want to discuss her symptoms and maybe examine her first."

"Oh, I see. All right, I'll tell her that, but I don't think she'll want to talk about her problem. I know she won't want to be examined."

Hearing affection and tolerance in the older woman's voice, Layla decided Zora probably *was* speaking for someone else. Not that it mattered. "There is one thing she could try without having to have a prescription."

"What's that?"

"It's a lubricant. Come to think of it, Majid has some. It's sold in tubes for home use, but doctors get it in little packets. They use it for rectal and vaginal exams. If you can wait a few minutes, I'll get you some when Majid finishes with his patient."

"Really? That would be wonderful, but Majid mustn't know about this. My sister-in-law would be mortified."

"Don't worry. I'll sneak into the examining room while you're talking to him. I'll just take a few packets—he won't miss them—and then I'll check around to see if any of the pharmacies carry it so your sister-in-law can buy more if she likes it." She explained to Zora how the lubricant could be used to alleviate vaginal dryness.

Majid gave them a questioning look as he walked with a young mother and her baby from the examining room toward the waiting room.

"Salaam, Mother," he said when he came back to the office. "What brings you here today?"

"Oh I just stopped by to say hello to Layla, dear. We've been having a nice chat."

Layla stood. "I'll get you that glass of water you wanted, Zora." She hurried past Majid before he could offer to get it himself. When she came back she handed Zora a paper cup full of water and dropped three packets of lubricant into the older woman's lap.

The next day, her work on the proposal was interrupted by a call from Zora. "Excuse me for bothering you," the older woman said. "I got your number from Majid. I hope you don't mind."

Layla assured Zora that it was no trouble at all.

"I hate to ask this, but my sister-in-law is quite enthusiastic about that stuff you gave her and she does want more. She'd be embarrassed to buy it herself. Can you get it for her? She'll pay, of course."

Layla chuckled and agreed to go to the pharmacy to make the purchase for the mystery sister-in-law. Zora said she would come by the clinic later in the afternoon to pick it up.

Layla donned her chador and went out to the reception area. "Tell Majid I'm taking a little break," she said to Saba. "I'm going to walk for a bit and do some shopping; I'll be back in an hour or so."

"Yes, khanoum." Saba had been very respectful ever since Layla delivered Darya's baby.

Layla walked to the pharmacy that sold her the ovulation kit.

The same clerk, the one with the thick glasses, helped her again. She held her chador across the lower half of her face when she asked if they had vaginal lubricant. He didn't seem to understand her request.

"It might be sold under the brand name, "KY Jelly," she suggested. When the puzzled expression remained on his face, she added, in a hushed voice, "It's used during sex."

"Oh." A flush of embarrassment colored his cheeks. "KY Jelly."

Thank goodness her chador hid the color she felt rise to her face. She must be absorbing the prudishness of the culture around her. She forced confidence into her voice when she answered, "Yes. KY Jelly."

"Of course, khanoum." All professional now, he found a tube and she bought it.

On the way back to the clinic, she stopped at a gift shop and bought a little figurine of a woman holding a baby. Later, back at the clinic, she showed it to Majid. "This is for your mother, a reminder of the lovely birth we witnessed together."

"That's very thoughtful of you. I'm sure she'll treasure it. Do you want me to take it to her?"

"I think she might be stopping by the clinic today. I'll give it to her then."

Majid was with a patient when Zora arrived half an hour later. Layla gave her the figurine.

Zora turned it over and over in her hands. "It's beautiful." She found a handkerchief in her purse and wiped at her eyes. "Thank you, dear. You didn't have to do this."

"I'm pleased to have found something for you. I hope it will remind you of Darya's birth and of me."

"Oh, darling girl, I'm sure I will never forget that birth. And I will never forget you. Nor will Majid." Sadness in her voice made Layla feel sad too. It was going to be hard to say goodbye to this country, to the people she'd met. To Majid.

She handed Zora the tube of lubrication and told her the name of the pharmacy where she'd bought it. "For all I know, every pharmacy in Behruz City carries it. Your sister-in-law might want to try another one closer to her home. But anyway, you can tell her the big pharmacy north of here by the park has it for sure."

"I don't think she'll be willing to ask for it herself, but I'll tell her. Thank you, dear."

Zora left without seeing Majid. Later, Layla told him his mother had come and had loved the little figurine. "I need to get a few more gifts," she told him. "For my family. Since they all have roots in Behruz, I'd like to find things that are really unique to this culture, but of course I can't get big things like samovars and carpets. Whatever I buy will have to fit in my suitcase. Maybe some kind of antique knick-knacks or religious artifacts. Do you have any idea where I might find something like that?"

"How about the antique bazaar? It's in the old part of the city, next to the main bazaar where food and household goods are sold."

"That will be perfect. Do you want to come with me?"

He chuckled under his breath. "Yes, Layla, I want to come with you."

They made plans to meet at the clinic Saturday morning.

****

127

When Majid arrived at the clinic for the trip to the bazaar, Layla was already there. Her T-shirt showed a stork carrying a baby, under which were the words, *If only it were that easy.*

He said, "Right. If only it *were* that easy." They smiled their shared awareness of how difficult childbirth can be.

There would be no parking in the market area, Majid explained, so they took a taxi. The narrow streets were so choked with cars, people, bicycles, and animals, the driver had to drop them off two blocks from the antique bazaar. They walked the rest of the way on a sidewalk that was as congested as the street: with street vendors, children, and a mass of moving humanity. Majid took Layla's hand. It was necessary, really; the risk of losing her in the crowd was real. Excitement and pleasure vibrated from her hand to his. Her fingers wrapped around his in a caress that sent shivers of longing through his body.

The bazaar was a huge dome-covered maze of narrow passageways lined with stalls. Some of the stalls had only a single bare bulb, and only a little light passed through dirty windows in the ceiling to illuminate the passageway.

The dimness where they walked and the river of humanity streaming around them made the place feel ominous. "Welcome to the Casbah," Majid said. They clung to each other, hands tightly clasped, both foreigners in this strange world.

He shouldn't be touching her. What would people think? What if he saw one of his patients?

He didn't care. She didn't seem to mind; that was all that mattered. He lifted her hand and studied its pale softness. "The henna is gone. Now can you tell me where you had a hidden tattoo?"

Her answering smile dazzled him. "On my belly. I had flower petals circling my belly button."

He pictured her bare belly: smooth and soft and painted with the petals of a flower. Desire jolted through his body.

"I see. Or, that is, I would love to *have seen...*" He cleared his throat. "Okay, let's go find you some Behruzi treasures." He led her along the passageway deeper into the bazaar.

The crowds and Layla's fascination with everything she saw made progress slow. A boy carrying a rolled rug on his shoulder swerved in front of them. The end of the rug struck Layla's shoulder, throwing her against Majid. He tightened his grip. "Are you all right?"

"Yes. It was nothing. I love this." She beamed her pleasure. They walked through the carpet section, which went on for the length of a city block, and then entered a section of used clothing, much of it apparently from the United States. Next was the furniture area, which was crammed with everything from worthless, banged-up Formica tables to exquisite French antiques. That was followed by a section where polished brass gleamed from every shelf. Here were the samovars she couldn't take back—and oil lamps and candleholders and ornate pitchers with long spouts. The pitchers were *aftebehs*, Majid explained. In places that didn't have indoor plumbing, *aftebehs* full of water were kept beside the toilet for cleansing.

Layla's eyes gleamed with delight. Seen through her eyes, his own country seemed exotic and fascinating. He felt ownership of it: it was his gift to her. His chest expanded; her hand in his made him feel powerful.

"Oh look." She pulled him toward a display of camel bells. This brass wasn't polished and shining; it had turned a mellow brownish gold with age. "I remember hearing the bell from the garbage man's camel when I was a little girl. It's one of my most vivid memories. I bet Rashid and Salma remember too. I'm going to get one for each of them."

"They're heavy," Majid cautioned. "Are you sure you want them in your luggage?"

"I may regret it by the time I get home, but I have to have them."

After much deliberation, she selected three bells, one for each of her siblings. "My younger sister doesn't remember much about our life in Behruz, but she'll want one too."

Majid had released her hand while she was selecting the bells, but when they were ready to leave, he took it again. He held her purchases in one hand and her delicate, unadorned fingers in the other as they continued down the crowded corridor toward the jewelry section.

She stopped at a stall selling nomad jewelry and was soon bent over a basket full of bracelets with little bells hanging from them. "Ankle bracelets," she said. "Olivia has a pair of these. Rashid bought them for her." She fingered them reverently and selected a pair. "I'll get these for Olivia's new baby."

Majid took one of the anklets into his hand and studied the delicate bells, imagining the craftsman who made them. He saw an old man in a village bazaar, someone who'd been a silversmith all his life, hammering the silver, soldering the fine details on each bell, and assembling and polishing the final piece. The result was whimsical and beautiful and an embodiment of a culture that was almost lost. A culture that was in Layla's blood just as it was in his.

"Let me buy you a pair," he said.

"Oh, no I couldn't."

"They've brought such delight to your eyes; please don't deny me the pleasure of giving you a pair."

She hesitated. "I do love them."

"Then it's settled. Which ones will it be?"

Most seemed to have been made for babies or small children, but Layla found several pairs that would fit her slender ankles. She picked out three to try on. The shopkeeper, an old man wearing loose nomad clothing and a turban, found a chair for her and a stool for Majid. Majid bent to secure a bracelet on one of her ankles.

His hands shook as he worked the rustic clasp. His face was inches from her knee; his knuckles grazed the flesh of her ankle. It was delight and torture combined.

"Can you roll up the leg of my jeans?" she asked. "I want to see."

He did as she asked, doubling the fabric slowly, savoring each millimeter of her flesh as it was revealed and letting his fingers linger a fraction of a second longer than necessary at each touch. She stretched out her leg and admired the result. "Beautiful. I think I want this pair, but I have to try the others too."

When she'd tried them all, she picked up the first pair again. She jiggled it beside her ear, her head cocked and her eyes closed, listening to its quiet music.

"Yes, these."

Majid's heart swelled with pleasure as if he'd presented her with the finest of the crown jewels.

The shopkeeper wrapped the baby-sized ankle bracelets in newspaper and tied the bundle with string. When he prepared to wrap the ones Layla had chosen for herself, she stopped him. "No, wait. I want to wear them."

Majid rolled up the other pant leg and secured bracelets on each of her ankles. Working the clasps required concentration, and so did containing his libido.

Soon they were walking along the narrow passageway again. Layla's hand was once again nestled in his, and her ankle bracelets jingled softly with each step.

She found a carved wooden ship for her nephew Jamie and an amber necklace for her mother.

The shopkeeper who sold the amber, a dark-skinned young woman dressed entirely in red with a flowered scarf over her hair, said, "The amber in our country was brought here in the time of Genghis Khan and has been worn for centuries by Behruzi women." She showed her how the beads had been worn flat where they rubbed together.

"What a beautiful girl," Layla remarked as they walked away with her purchase. "Is she a nomad?"

"No, I believe she's a gypsy, a member of a group called *the Dom* who have settled throughout the Middle East."

"Do you think the amber I bought is really as old as she said?"

"I wouldn't be surprised. Amber had to be brought here from somewhere. It comes from the sea, so it couldn't have been found in Behruz."

"Do people still wear it?"

"Only those who cling to the old ways: nomads, gypsies, and a few women in the villages. It's believed to have magical properties."

When they emerged from the dark labyrinth of the bazaar onto a street on the other side, they decided to have lunch in Ferdowsi Park. Majid found a taxi.

The park was almost as crowded as the bazaar. There were children everywhere, running on the pathways and playing in the grass. There were a few other Westerners, mostly women with Behruzi husbands. None of the other foreign women wore chadors. Layla took hers off and carried it folded over her arm.

Majid bought piroshkies and pomegranate juice from a vendor, and found an unoccupied bench. Layla's eyes were on the activity around them as she ate. Eager children stood in line a few feet away, each one clutching the needed coins, waiting to buy a balloon from the balloon vendor.

"I'm going to miss all this," Layla said.

Did she mean she was going to miss him? He searched her eyes for the answer, but her gaze skittered away.

"Less than a week," she said.

"Five days," he said.

A little girl chased a balloon as it bounced along the pathway in front of them, and a boy a few years older ran after her. Layla looked at the children and then up at the cypress trees that shaded them. She sighed.

"How's your aunt doing?" Majid asked. "Is the

wait driving her crazy?"

Layla swallowed the last bite of her piroshky. "Yes."

"Does she have any symptoms of pregnancy?"

"I'm dying to know, but I don't ask because I'm afraid speculating about it will add to her craziness. She did mention breast tenderness, so I'm hopeful."

"It will be a stroke of luck if she gets pregnant on the first try."

"Yes, I know. I keep telling her and my uncle that, but they're really counting on having success while I'm here. Good things tend to fall into her lap with very little effort on her part, so maybe she'll be lucky in this too."

He liked seeing her out in the open with no chador. He motioned to it where it lay next to them on the bench. "You don't have to wear that thing all the time, you know. We're used to seeing foreign women without them. Behruzi women are becoming more relaxed about using them too."

"I know. I've seen a few Behruzi women here in the park wearing just scarves instead of chadors. I don't know; I don't like to stand out. It was important to me to fit in when I first went to the States."

"Well, you've become a vibrant, talented and beautiful woman. I can't imagine it's as important to fit in now as it was then."

She blushed and smiled. "Maybe I am changing in that regard. This time in Behruz has made me feel—it's hard to describe—kind of like I've lost my moorings, like things that used to make me feel secure don't work as well as they once did. I feel lost sometimes, but then at other times I think something deeper is emerging."

Majid held his breath, waiting for her to say more. *Something deeper emerging. Something that could take the place of what she'd once needed.*

He wanted the thing she no longer needed to be that damned fiancé in Texas.

He wanted her to confide in him, to share every step of discovery. "That must be exciting," he said.

"Yes. Exciting and a little scary."

"Well, scary can be good."

"Yes. But scary can also be *scary*."

He shouldn't ask. He shouldn't ask. He shouldn't ask…

He did ask—with a shaking voice. "Does this affect how you feel about your fiancé?"

She smiled a tremulous little smile. "No. Dan is the one unchanging constant in my life."

Majid's heart clunked to a stop.

His litany, like a rap song, played again in his head. *She's an American. She's engaged. She's leaving in five days.*

Chapter Eleven

Zora came to the office again the next day.

"Salaam," she said to Layla. "Am I interrupting your work?"

Layla arched her back and stretched her arms. "No, not at all. Have a seat."

The older woman sat opposite Layla, smiling an apology. "I'm here to ask another favor."

"I'll be happy to help if I can. What is it?"

"Well, two of my sisters-in-law heard about the medicine you bought for my other sister-in-law, and they want to try it too. And one of them has a sister who wants to try it. So they were wondering if you could go to the pharmacy for them again…" Her cheeks colored, but she forged on. "They were hoping you might get a little extra since after you leave there won't be anyone to buy it. They'll pay, of course. They've all given me money."

Layla laughed. She couldn't help it. The image of those conservative older women, all excited to try a vaginal lubricant, was just too funny. Zora looked alarmed, but then she laughed too.

"Is this by any chance going to be for any of the aunts I've met?"

Zora took a linen handkerchief from her purse and wiped her eyes. "I can't name names, of course, but let's just say that if you ever have a chance to visit my father-in-law's home again, you'll receive a more friendly welcome."

They laughed even harder.

They went together to the pharmacy. Zora waited in the taxi while Layla, with her chador hiding most of her face, went in to make the purchase. "How can I help you today?" her old friend with the thick glasses asked in a voice that was cool and professional but with an emphasis on the word *today* that made it clear he remembered her purchase of KY Jelly a few days earlier.

She met his eyes, her heart hammering as if she were a timid Behruzi virgin, not a sophisticated midwife from the U.S., and said, "I would like seven tubes of KY Jelly, please."

He did a double-take. "Seven tubes of what?"

"KY Jelly." She enunciated clearly. She didn't falter in her eye contact. "Please."

"Oh, yes, of course." He disappeared into the back of the store and returned with the seven tubes. He probably thought she was running a brothel.

"And do you have a home pregnancy test?" It had occurred to her that it would be nice to test in the privacy of Abu-Khan's chambers before they went to the lab for the blood test.

The pharmacist's eyebrows curved into a quizzical arch. He was probably trying to picture what kind of life would require seven tubes of KY Jelly while the possibility of pregnancy loomed.

He said yes, they did have home pregnancy test kits. She said she wanted one, and he found it in the back of the store.

"Thank you," she said. She gave him the money

and took the receipt. She held her head high as she walked out the door.

"It was a bit harrowing," she told Zora when she got into the taxi, "but mission accomplished."

"On behalf of my sisters-in-law, I thank you." Zora placed her hand over Layla's. "Their husbands will never know their indebtedness to you, but I thank you on their behalf too."

"These women should see a doctor about possibly getting some estrogen cream or hormone replacement therapy, but if they won't do that, they can keep using this stuff. Tell them to get their husbands to buy it."

Zora chuckled. "I don't think the women would be willing to ask that of their husbands."

"Well then, tell them to put on a chador, march into a pharmacy, and ask for what they want. The pharmacy sells the stuff; that means your sisters-in-law aren't the only people in Behruz using it."

"All right, dear. I'll tell them that's what you advised."

They went to an open-air café for tea.

Zora dropped three cubes of sugar into tea that was already as sweet as maple syrup. "I'm sorry you have to leave so soon, Layla. Are you sure you can't stay in Behruz a little longer?"

"No, I really have to get back. I already have my airline reservation, and my fiancé is getting impatient."

"Oh, of course. Yes. You're getting married. I'm sorry, dear. It's selfish of me, but I can't help wishing you didn't have to go. I'll miss you, and I know Majid will too. But if you're sure…"

She *was* sure, wasn't she? Zora's kind words confused her, making her mind and heart veer into frightening territory. But she mustn't let fear and doubt take hold. She took a deep breath. She tried to bring Dan's image to mind—his strength and certainty—but they evaded her. Still, in an effort to make it true, she said, "Yes, Zora. I'm sure."

Zora dropped Layla off at the clinic and then kept the taxi for her trip home.

Majid stopped into the office an hour later to have tea with Layla between patients. "Saba said my mother was here."

"Yes. She just wanted to say goodbye. We went for a little walk."

"Really? But you're not leaving until Thursday."

"I probably won't have another chance to see her."

"Oh right. Of course."

Some cosmic fast-forward button had been pushed, and her time in Behruz was running out so quickly she couldn't keep up. She wanted everything to slow down. She wanted to savor each moment: each walk together, each shared meal, each glance and smile from him. She imagined excuses for him to take her hand again. Maybe now, she thought when they crossed the street together. Or now—when he was saying goodnight at the end of the day. *Take my hand. Put your arms around me. Kiss me. Take me.*

No. Where had that come from? This trip had stirred things up in her. Majid had stirred things up. Both her body and her mind were unsettled.

She wanted to stay. But maybe leaving was best. When she saw Dan again, her world would settle back to normal.

That evening at dinner, Abu-Khan said he'd spoken to Olivia.

Finally. The poor man had tortured himself for a week before calling. Layla studied his face for clues as to how the conversation had gone.

He was smiling a soft smile she'd never seen on his face. He looked younger. "It was good," he said.

Bless Olivia's kind heart. "I'm happy to hear that."

Abu-Khan's face sobered. "Surely we can perform the pregnancy test now?"

Did he think Olivia's forgiveness made a possible pregnancy somehow magically advance enough to show up on a test?

Mina's mouth assumed a sad, little pout. "Please, Layla?"

Layla explained for the tenth time that testing too early could give erroneous results. She felt sympathy for both of them, but she mustered up a stern tone when she spoke to Abu-Khan. "You need to help Mina relax and be patient during this wait."

Finally, on Wednesday, it was time to test. Mina called when she woke up and Layla hurried to the royal chambers to help with the home pregnancy test. Abu-Khan sat in his robe, fiddling with prayer beads instead of his hair, while the two women went into the bathroom together. Three minutes later they hugged happily. With tears streaming down her face, Mina ran out to tell Abu-Khan.

He stood, dropping the beads to the floor. "Am I going to have a baby? A real baby of my own? Can I announce it?"

Layla laughed. "It appears that *Mina* is going to have a baby, and yes it will be real and it will be *yours*. We'll confirm it with a blood test today and then again in a few days. You should wait at least until after the second blood test before announcing it, Abu-Khan. Many people wait three months—until the risk of miscarriage is pretty much over."

"We have to have a second blood test in a few days? But you won't be here then," Abu-Khan complained.

"You won't need me anymore. From now on this will be a normal pregnancy. Mina can go to any lab in the city for the second blood test, and her mother can go with her. You can have your own doctors come to the palace to treat Mina from now on. No one will question how she conceived."

"Oh, I see." Doubt alternated with hope on his face. He turned away; and a gasping moan exploded from his lips.

Mina shifted from one foot to the other and glanced uncertainly at Layla. "Go to your husband," Layla whispered. "Hold him."

Mina put one arm around Abu-Khan's waist and rested her cheek awkwardly against his chest. He threw his arms around her and buried his face in her hair. Layla crept quietly from the room.

She called Majid to tell him the news and then ate breakfast. When she was done, she called the royal chambers using the intercom system and made plans to go with Mina to the lab for the blood test. Once again, during the taxi drive and at the lab, they hid their identities with their chadors. Layla asked the lab to do the work immediately, and Mina pulled a fat wad of bills from her purse to pay for the expedited service.

When the blood test confirmed Mina was pregnant, they went from the lab to Majid's clinic to share the good news with him.

141

"Thank you, thank you, thank you," Mina, still hidden, said to both of them.

"I'm very happy for you," Layla said. Majid added his congratulations.

"I remember when I thought you were the one who was hoping to get pregnant," he said to Layla.

"I wish you would forget. I'm sorry I lied to you."

"It was my husband's fault," Mina said.

Layla asked Mina to have lunch with them, but Mina wanted to tell Abu-Khan the good news.

Layla and Majid had lunch at his desk—*one last time*—and Layla prepared to go back to the palace. The proposal was finished and had been translated and sent to the Health Department. There was nothing more she could do.

"Can I take you to the airport tomorrow?" Majid asked.

Layla couldn't bear the thought of saying goodbye at the airport. "It won't be necessary. My uncle has it all arranged."

"I see."

They stared at each other across the desk. Layla's heart was breaking, but there was nothing she could say. She loved Dan. The wedding plans were all in place. She'd bought a dress. Salma's daughter was excited about being a flower girl. And she had all those shower gifts. The feelings she had for Majid were just friendship. And respect and admiration and a deep affection. Maybe infatuation...

She pressed her fingers against her temples and closed her eyes, squeezing them tight. What was happening? This was too hard.

Majid was gazing at her, very still, waiting.

She dropped her hands to her lap and rubbed the finger that should have held her engagement ring. She had no right to leave him with unanswered questions. It would be wrong. He didn't deserve it. So she squared her shoulders and said what she needed to say. "This is hard, but I've been gone a long time. My fiancé is getting impatient."

Majid sat up straighter too. "Yes, of course."

"So, I guess it's time to say goodbye."

Majid cleared his throat, but still his voice came out gruff. "Right. But... Let me take you to dinner tonight."

She twisted her ringless fingers together and whispered the word she knew she shouldn't say. "Yes."

Back at the palace, Omid accosted her as soon as she stepped through the main entrance. Where had she been? What had she been doing? Abu-Khan wanted to see her. *Right now.*

She ran to the elevator and rushed down the hallway. Was it Mina? Was there a problem with the pregnancy?

Abu-Khan asked the same questions Omid had: where had she been, and what had she been doing? Layla ignored him as she had Omid. "What is it Abu-Khan?"

He was standing in the middle of the room. He ran his fingers through his hair. "Sit down," he said.

Layla sat in an upholstered chair in the corner next to Mina. "Are you all right, Mina?"

The younger girl smiled timidly. "Yes, I'm fine."

Abu-Khan still stood. He was no longer the man who'd broken down with emotion the day before. Now he was the imperious sultan. "You can't leave tomorrow. Mina needs you."

Layla spoke to Mina, not Abu-Khan. "I'm sorry, honey. I have to go tomorrow. I have a lot to do to get ready for a move and a wedding, and I already have my airline reservation. It can't be changed. You're going to be fine. You're young and healthy. From now on this will be a normal pregnancy."

"I'll pay to change your reservation," Abu-Khan said.

Mina stuck out her lower lip in a pouty frown. "Please?"

Layla glared a warning at Abu-Khan before speaking gently to Mina, "You don't need me. You'll have another blood test in a few days and maybe one more after that, but then all you need to do is eat well, get plenty of rest, and see a doctor once a month."

"But what if something goes wrong?" Abu-Khan whined.

"You'll call the doctor, Abu-Khan."

"What about your precious project that takes you away from the palace every day? How can you leave that?"

"I've finished with the first stage. There's nothing more to do until the approval comes through from the Health Department. That will take months, maybe a year—if they even do approve it."

"What if the approval came through more quickly? What if it came through today? Then would you have a reason to stay?"

Today? Her heart quickened. Oh what that would mean to Majid. Could it really happen today?

She'd be able to help with the grant application. She'd already had ideas for the curriculum of the training. What fun it would be to develop those ideas.

If she stayed a little longer.

No. Dan would never understand. He might not forgive her.

But...

Abu-Khan was waiting. Her heart blurted an answer before her mind could decide. "Maybe I could stay a few weeks more. *If* the approval came through today."

Abu-Khan and Mina shared one of their newlywed smiles. "That's all I ask," Abu-Khan said.

"This project is important, Abu-Khan. Your helping it along is a good thing."

He smiled an uncertain smile. "Olivia made me promise to find ways to help women and children in Behruz. Would this count?"

Bless Olivia. "Yes, Abu-Khan, it would. I'll tell Olivia what you've done. But please keep in mind that I absolutely, positively must be in San Francisco three weeks from now. I've promised to be there to deliver Olivia and Rashid's baby."

"I understand. I'll explain to Omid. He'll have one of my secretaries change your reservation."

This was happening too fast. "I should check with my fiancé."

"Surely he won't care about a few more weeks."

Layla prayed Abu-Khan was right as she went upstairs to get her flight information and took it down to Omid. She couldn't call Dan now: he'd be asleep. She'd call him tonight. Oh how she dreaded it.

But the problem of telling Dan slipped from her mind as she unpacked. All she could think of now was: *she had to tell Majid.*

She wanted to tell him in person. She would wait until dinner.

Chapter Twelve

Majid locked the front door of the clinic and stepped onto the sidewalk. He said good evening to Mohammed. Then he waited. For Layla. For his last dinner with her, his last chance to see her, his last chance to tell her how he felt.

His last chance to kiss her.

He could kiss her without revealing his feelings, couldn't he? A goodbye kiss. Something casual. That would seem like a normal act of friendship, wouldn't it?

One kiss at the end of the evening. And then she would leave, as American women did, and he would get on with his life.

He saw her coming toward him when she was almost a block away. Apparently she'd walked from wherever it was her uncle lived. She was moving fast; her chador, which was loosely draped over her head, flew back behind her, revealing that she'd dressed especially for the occasion. She was wearing a long skirt, a satin top with a scooped neck, strappy sandals—and the ankle bracelets. Her hair was soft and loose around her shoulders. Happy energy radiated from her.

When she got to the clinic, she greeted Mohammed first and then said, "Good evening, Majid."

His arms wanted to reach for her. He put his hands in his pockets. "Good evening, Layla. You look lovely."

"Thank you. Can we go inside before we head for the restaurant? There's something I want to tell you."

She grinned. Her cocky, cheerful spirit seemed undiminished. Didn't she feel any of the distress he felt about saying goodbye? He told her he had something to tell her as well.

"You go first," she said when they were seated on chairs in the waiting room.

"The most amazing thing has happened. Approval for the doula project has come through from the Health Department. I don't know how it happened so fast; it's totally unprecedented. I thought you'd want to know I'll be going forward with the grant application."

"Oh, that's wonderful. And it relates to my news." She didn't show as much surprise as he expected. Of course, she didn't have any experience with the snail-paced workings of Behruzi bureaucracy, but still, even in the States, an approval such as this would take at least weeks, probably months.

"Yes?" Her eyes sparkled and her face glowed. This was how he would remember her.

"I'm not leaving tomorrow."

"What?"

"My uncle has convinced me to stay three weeks longer. I have to be back for the birth of my brother's baby, but I'm going to stay until I have to leave for that. My uncle is paying for the new airline ticket. I can help you with the grant application if you like."

Majid hadn't taken a breath since she said the words, *not leaving tomorrow*. Now he gulped in air, stunned. Three more weeks. He reached impulsively for her hands. He held them and caressed them with his thumbs and gazed into her gleaming eyes. "That is wonderful news."

She squeezed his hands. Her smiling lips and smiling eyes were radiant. He struggled to resist the urge to take her in his arms.

He kept her hand in his as they walked to the Chinese restaurant.

They found a table and ordered their meals. Majid asked, "Have you told your fiancé?"

"No. I'll call him tonight. He's going to be pretty unhappy with me."

A flicker of smug satisfaction flashed through Majid as he thought of the American's disappointment.

They talked about the grant application. Layla said, "I can't wait to get started."

"Thank goodness you're going to be here to do it. I'd never have found anyone half as qualified as you to help with it."

Watching her gracefully maneuver the chopsticks, listening to her sweet, soft voice propose ideas for the grant application, knowing he had three more weeks to hear her voice and work with her, was such a reprieve, such a miracle, Majid's heart was nearly bursting with the pleasure of it. Listening to her and watching her, he was spellbound. Back out on the sidewalk after the meal, when it was time to find her a taxi and say goodnight, he found he wasn't ready to break the spell. He said, "I have to go back to the clinic to get my car. Walk with me. We'll get you a taxi there."

"All right."

He took her hand again. He shouldn't. Nothing had changed. She was still going back to marry her American fiancé. But it felt natural. How could it be wrong?

They stood alone in front of the clinic, facing each other, their hands still linked. The street was quiet, the neighborhood shops were closed, and Mohammed had gone. They were in darkness except for soft light from a streetlamp at the corner.

Three weeks stretched out before him like the three months of summer vacation when he was in school. But the goodbye kiss he'd imagined just a few hours ago was now three weeks away as well. Looking down at her, at her soft lips and melting eyes, he couldn't bear to wait. Yearning overcame caution. He said, "There were two things I planned to do tonight when I thought you were leaving tomorrow."

"Yes?"

"Well, first, I was going to give you a gift. It's inside if you want it now."

Her eyes lit up. "Of course I want it now."

He unlocked the front door and they went in. His heart was hammering. Layla sat in the waiting room while he went back to his office for the gift.

He watched with trembling anticipation as she pulled at the giftwrap and opened the package.

"Oh, the Persian poet Rumi. I love him." She slid her fingers along the brocaded silk cover of the book and opened it to the title page where Majid had written simply his name.

She flipped through the pages, stopping where he'd left a bookmark. He held his breath as her fingers skimmed along lines he'd lightly underlined.

*You are rest for my soul,*
*A surprising joy…*
*Imagination has never imagined*
*What you give to me.*

She looked up finally, her eyes glistening, her lips compressed. She closed the book and clutched it to her heart. "It's beautiful. I don't know what to say."

"Don't say anything." He'd had to tell her how he felt, or let Rumi do it for him, but he didn't expect her to answer with the words he longed to hear. It was better that she say nothing.

"Thank you."

"You're welcome."

She was still going back to America to marry her blond Adonis.

"I have the same book in Farsi," he said. "I felt pretty lucky to find a copy for you in English."

"I'll treasure it forever." She still held the book pressed to her heart. "You mentioned there were two things you wanted to do…"

"Oh, yes." His heart lurched in his throat, but he continued. "The other thing was…I was going to kiss you. It would have been a casual, chaste kiss, of course. A friendly goodbye kiss."

Fire sparked in her eyes. "That won't be necessary now that I'm staying."

That fire looked like flirtation. It looked like longing. His heart raced. "Right. It's not strictly necessary. But the thing is, I've sort of warmed to the idea of doing it. I'm having a little trouble adjusting to the idea of *not* doing it."

She tilted her head to the side, looking coy and adorable. "In that case, since you haven't been able to adjust to the idea of *not* doing it, perhaps instead of a goodbye kiss, a friendly, glad-you're-not-leaving kiss would be in order. A *chaste* glad-you-re-not-leaving kiss, of course."

"Well if that's what you think is best..." He reached for her hands and pulled her to her feet. *Keep it light. A friendly, kidding-around kiss.* Her grin faded. She placed her hand flat on his chest, sparking tingles of anticipation. Her eyes smoldered; she swayed toward him. Could he keep it chaste and light-hearted? Could he hold back his feelings?

Yes, he could. He had to.

She was only inches away from him. Her body, her face, her lips. *Her lips.* Layla's precious lips. He touched them with shaking fingers. Layla, Layla, Layla. He rested his hands on her shoulders and bent toward her, his heart thudding. She tilted up her face, and he placed his lips where his fingers had been. Current vibrated between them. Her lips parted, just slightly, and his did too. It was a reverent kiss; their lips moved against each other as if they'd been kissing for a lifetime. Her lips were soft. Her body would be soft. He could pull her toward him—she seemed to be as lost in the kiss as he was—it would take no effort at all.

What would take effort, what *did* take effort, was stopping.

But he did.

She was still engaged.

Or was she? He had to ask. "Are you having second thoughts about your wedding?"

"Oh." She pulled back from him. Her eyes skittered away. "Oh. I forgot."

He dropped his hands. He tried not to sound accusing. "You're surprisingly able to compartmentalize your life."

It had sounded accusing. And so did his next words: "When you get back to the States, are you going to forget me?"

Her face crumpled as if he'd slapped her. She looked down at the floor. "No. Never."

Looking at the top of her head, he saw a single white hair snaking its way through the dark waves. "Tell me, Layla, how are you going to remember me?"

"I don't know. Don't make me say it."

He crossed his arms to keep from reaching for her again. "Don't make you say what? How you feel? Do you know how you feel, Layla? Sometimes I think you don't even know who you are."

She balled her fists. "It's easy for you, with your big family of purebred Behruzis, to know who you are and what you want. You don't know what it was like to be uprooted and made to adapt overnight to a completely different culture."

"You seem to have forgotten that I did spend ten years in your country."

"Oh, that's right... But I was a child when it happened to me."

"Yes, you were a child, but you had a mother, an *American* mother, to help ease the way. I was completely alone."

She sat down, and he did too. She stared at her hands, kneading them together in her lap. "Yes, I had a mother, but she'd just lost her husband, and life didn't slow down to let her grieve: she had to move four children halfway around the world."

He put his arm around her shoulders. "I'm sorry. That must have been a difficult time for all of you. How did your father die?"

She nestled her cheek against the crook of his elbow. "He had a heart attack. It was sudden."

153

"What about your older brother and sister? Didn't they help you adjust to life in America?"

"They'd just lost their father, so they were pretty preoccupied with their own loss. And they were adolescents in a new school. New kids with Muslim names. Rashid had always been my strongest supporter, but he was having an especially hard time. He was pretty much lost to me when I needed him most."

"I see. You'd lost your father too. How did that affect you?"

"I don't know. Everything in my life changed practically overnight. I was just trying to survive."

"I suppose your father is buried here in Behruz. Have you been to his grave site?"

Color drained from her face. She lifted her head and sat up straighter. "No. I never thought of it. I should go! I don't think I ever said goodbye to him. Maybe I saw him after he died, before the funeral, but I don't have any memory of it. I felt like he just disappeared. I think I felt abandoned by him." Her eyes brimmed with tears. She whispered. "Later, when we got to the States, I felt like *I had abandoned him*."

"Do you know where he's buried?"

"No, but my uncle will know."

"Find out where he is. I'll take you."

\*\*\*\*

Dan answered the phone on the first ring. "Hi, darlin'. I can't talk long. I have a meeting with the athletic director this morning."

"Okay. I'll try to hurry then. There's something I need to tell you."

"It's an important meeting, Layla. We're going to discuss next year's budget. I'm hoping to get new uniforms and more money for recruiting."

"That would be great, Dan." Oh God, he wasn't going to take this well, but she had to tell him. She blurted it out. "The thing is…I'm not leaving Behruz tomorrow."

A chill came through the airwaves. "What did you say?"

"I'm sorry. I'm staying three more weeks. Abu-Khan has convinced me. His wife is pregnant, and she thinks she can't make it through the first few weeks without me." It sounded lame. It was lame. "And the Health Department approval came through for the doula project, so I'll be able to work on the grant application." Had she even told him about the doula project? She thought she had, but she wasn't sure he'd really listened.

"What on earth are you talking about? What do you mean you won't be here for three more weeks? Layla, you promised…"

She hadn't exactly *promised*, had she?

He went on whining his disappointment. He already had to find an apartment on his own and start furnishing it on his own, and it was embarrassing to have to keep explaining why she wasn't with him for important events at the college. The sultan's wife was pregnant? So what? They did have doctors in Behruz, didn't they? How could events in that godforsaken country be more important than starting her life with Dan?

He had a right to be angry. Her change of plans was a tremendous betrayal. And he'd have a right to be angrier still when she explained she wasn't going immediately to Dallas. She was going to stay in San

Francisco until Olivia's baby made her appearance.

She should tell him now. But he was in a hurry to get to a meeting, and he was angry. She'd bring it up later when he was in a better mood.

"Does this mean we have to postpone the reception?"

"No, Dan. I'll get everything done. Don't worry; it's going to be beautiful. I'm so, so, so sorry about this, but it's just something I have to do."

"Have you already changed your reservation?"

"Yes." Omid had brought her the details of her new flight before she left for dinner with Majid.

"Then I guess there's nothing more to say. I have to go now. I need to get to the meeting—for the sake of my *career*. Fortunately, at least one of us is concerned about *our future*."

Layla lay in bed afterward feeling guilty about disappointing Dan and about not telling him everything. She should have mentioned Olivia's labor. And she should have told him about Majid's kiss.

Maybe she should wait to tell him about the kiss. She could explain it better in person.

Or maybe she didn't have to tell him about it at all. It was just a goodbye kiss. Well, a glad-you're-not-leaving kiss subbing for a goodbye kiss. A kiss of friendship. Making a formal confession out of it and trying to *explain* it would exaggerate its importance.

She and Majid were the only ones who could understand the friendship and respect that were expressed by that kiss. Friendship and respect and something deeper that didn't have a name, something that was so unique to her and Majid, no one else would understand. Dan would not understand. Better not to try.

She crawled into the luxury of her big bed and thought about having three more weeks to work on the project with Majid. Memories of the kiss crept into her thoughts. A liquid glow like warm honey hummed in her belly—and below her belly—when she thought of it. It radiated to her heart, feeling like…connection. And hope. She couldn't sleep.

She turned on the light and took the Rumi book from the bedside table. As she flipped through the pages, her eyes fell on the lines:

*I would love to kiss you.*
*The price of kissing is your life.*

The second line struck like a blow. Her life, everything she'd wanted and planned for, really was at stake. The kiss that was supposed to have been casual now seemed like a careless, stupid impulse. Shame engulfed her as she recalled how she'd invited that kiss.

She'd welcomed it.

She'd wanted it.

She was playing with fire.

Heat from that fire still tingled on her lips as she drifted into sleep.

Chapter Thirteen

Majid smiled at Layla as he passed the open door of his office. He smiled at his patient. He smiled at the world. Layla's presence in his office, intent on her work, on *their* work, still seemed like a miracle every time he saw her. Miracles abounded suddenly. First there was the approval of the doula project from the Health Department, and then, just two days ago, when he asked the hospital board if Layla could teach a course on labor support to the nurses, heads bobbed as if he'd just proposed offering big bonuses to everyone on staff. "Yes, of course," Dr. Mansur said. "That's a good idea."

It *was* a good idea. The course would accomplish two goals: it would strengthen the nurses' labor support skills, and teaching it would help Layla in her planning for the doula training. Still, Majid could scarcely believe Dr. Mansur was going along with it. As far as Majid knew, Dr. Mansur had never seen merit in anyone else's idea in his life.

What was happening to make the hospital board suddenly amenable to his ideas? It felt as if Layla were the talisman that cleared the way. How could that be?

Layla was thrilled. She was busy planning the curriculum for what would be a series of four two-hour classes. And when she wasn't working on that she was working on the grant application. She was determined to have it finished before she left.

Before she left in two and a half weeks.

Once again, Majid was counting.

\*\*\*\*

Layla leaned back into the comfortable upholstery of Majid's car and watched the sights streaming past. After driving for almost forty-five minutes, they were now in a poor part of the city where water ran in little channels along the sides of unpaved streets, and houses were made of mud bricks. There were fruit trees and flowering bushes growing in every patch of soil. Chickens scratched for food under the trees. Happy, barefoot children chased the chickens and each other and played in the streams that brought water to their homes.

She was wearing a chador over jeans and a T-shirt that proclaimed *Peace on earth begins with birth*. They were on their way, using directions provided by one of Abu-Khan's secretaries, to the cemetery where her father lay buried. It was a private cemetery in a neighborhood that had once been a small village but was now a suburb in the sprawl of Behruz City.

They passed through a slightly more prosperous area. Homes were crammed together with almost no yards, but they were made of real brick and had shingled roofs. Majid pulled the car over to the side of the road behind a donkey cart. "This must be it," he said.

Layla looked around. There was no cemetery in sight, just more houses and, ahead, a stone wall covered with vines.

"Behind that wall?" she asked.

"I think so."

They got out and went closer. Soon they found a little open doorway so low Majid had to duck to pass through it. Once inside, Layla gasped with delight. It was a small cemetery, about the size of a building lot back home, but it looked more like a garden. An enchanted garden: overgrown with weeds, partly shaded by trees, and littered with tombstones and pumpkins.

The pumpkin vines crawled over the tombstones and up the trunks of trees. Zucchini and tomato plants grew between the tombstones.

They followed a narrow path that led toward the center of the cemetery. A turbaned old man, barefoot and carrying a hoe, appeared from behind a tree laden with pomegranates.

The old man bowed solemnly. "Salaam alaikum."

Majid gave a slight bow and replied, "Salaam, esteemed elder. How are you?"

The man smiled a toothless smile and said he was well.

Majid asked, "Have you lived in this neighborhood long? Did you know the family whose ancestors rest here?"

"Yes, agha. I am Rafa Ali." He touched his forehead, indicating he was at their service. "I've lived here all my life. I kept these grounds and the family gardens for the old agha Shirvani until the day he died—may he rest in peace. I still take care of the cemetery, though not as well as I did when I was young, and I grow my vegetables here. Agha Shirvani gave me permission in his will to plant and harvest in this place as long as I live."

"Did you know my father, Darien Shirvani?" Layla

asked.

The old man looked at Layla as if he were seeing a ghost. "You are Darien Shirvani's daughter?"

"Yes, Agha. I've come from America. I want to visit my father's grave."

"Oh, dear girl, your father—may he rest in peace—used to follow me around when he was a boy, asking a million questions and trying to help. My, what a nuisance he was. But he grew into a fine man."

"Can you help us find his tombstone?"

"Yes, of course. I know exactly where it is. Follow me."

He set out down the path, using the hoe as a cane, and they followed him until he stopped in the far corner under the largest walnut tree Layla had ever seen.

A dim memory came to her. She remembered gathering walnuts under this tree. She remembered playing in this cemetery.

"Have I been here before, Agha? Did my father bring us here?"

"Yes, khanoum, your father brought you and your brother and sisters here several times. You used to hide from each other behind the tombstones."

"I remember."

The old man pointed with his hoe to a small, plain tombstone, which leaned a little to the side and was nearly covered by tall grass. "Here lies your father—may he rest in peace."

Layla went down on her knees and pulled the grass away so she could see the words carved into the stone. They were written in English. Her mother must have ordered the inscription.

*Darien Shirvani, 1958—1997*

*Beloved husband of Mary*
*And devoted father to*
*Salma, Rashid, Layla, and Suzi*

She'd been here with her father. This old man had seen them together as a happy family. It came back to her, not specific memories, but the feeling of being cherished and protected by her father.

She touched his name on the tombstone. "Oh Daddy, I miss you so much." She hadn't known how much she missed him. She hadn't known how much she lost when he died. Tears pooled in her eyes, and she let them flow. She let the feelings of pain and loss come out from where they'd been buried in her heart. Majid and the old man stood a few feet away, silently allowing her to grieve.

After a while, when her tears had dried, Majid said, "I brought a candle. Would you like to light it?"

"Oh yes." She tugged at the grass. Majid came down on his knees beside her to help, and the old man used his hoe to hack at weeds on the other side of the tombstone.

When they'd cleared the area, Majid produced a white candle and a package of matches. Leaning against the hoe and using his foot, the old man nudged a rock into place in front of the monument. Layla held the candle, and Majid lit it. She let wax drip onto the stone to form a little puddle and then settled the base of the candle into it. The old man intoned in Farsi, "May God hold you in the palm of his hand, dear child."

Layla whispered, "I love you, Daddy."

Majid stood and helped her to stand too. He put his arms around her, and she rested her head on his shoulder, on that place that had beckoned her before.

She felt at peace.

"Is there anyone left of my father's family?" she asked the old man.

"No, khanoum. Your father's parents died before you were born—may they rest in peace. His only uncle went to Canada when he was a young man and has never been heard of again. Their old home is still standing, but of course another family lives there now. It's only a few blocks from here. Do you want to see it?"

Did she? No. She shook her head. "This is the place I needed to see."

As they walked toward the street, Layla looked back at the candle until it was out of sight. *Goodbye, Daddy. I love you.*

Majid had brought food for them: skewered lamb and rice from Mohammed and soft drinks and fresh flatbread, thinking they might have a picnic in the cemetery. He offered it all to the old man, who accepted it with profuse expressions of gratitude and repeated assurances that he was "at their service."

"Thank you for bringing me," Layla said as they drove away.

Majid pulled her to him and nestled her head against his shoulder. She stayed that way, breathing in the soapy scent and strength of him, all the way back to the clinic.

****

Layla was nervous waiting for the class to begin. She'd taught similar classes back home, but this was the first time she'd be teaching in Farsi.

The classroom filled. There were about twenty nurses, mostly from Obstetrics but some from other

163

Judy Meadows

departments. Layla recognized a few of the faces from when she'd worked in the hospital.

After introducing herself, she said, "Today we're going to talk about the importance of childbirth in the life of a woman and in the life of a family. I want to go around the room and have each of you introduce yourself. If you have children, tell us about your labors."

The women all shifted in their seats and glanced uneasily at each other. Layla called on one of the nurses she remembered from the last labor she attended in the hospital. "Roksana, would you be willing to start us off?"

It took some coaxing, but Layla gently drew the woman out until she told about her first labor, which had ended in a cesarean, and a second birth, a planned cesarean.

"How do you feel about your experiences?" Layla asked.

Roksana looked down at her hands, which were clenched together in her lap. "My mother and my aunts and my mother-in-law all had natural births. I kind of feel like a failure, like I'm less of a woman than they are."

"I'm sorry you had to go through that, Roksana. Where did your older relatives have their babies?"

Roksana glanced around the room and then settled her eyes on Layla. "They've never really talked about it, but I assume they were in their homes. I think everyone had their babies at home back then."

"That's what I've heard. So, if they had their babies at home, they would have been surrounded by female relatives who helped and encouraged them. Do you think it would have made a difference to you if you'd had that kind of help?"

Roksana swiped at her eyes with a handkerchief and said, "Yes."

Layla said, "Studies show that when women are given emotional support during labor, they're less likely to end up with unwanted interventions, including cesareans. When unwanted interventions *are* needed, a woman is far less traumatized if she's been kept informed, if she feels heard, if she participates in the decision-making process, and if she has emotional support."

Heads nodded around the room.

Layla persuaded another woman to tell her story, which involved an equal sense of failure even though the birth ended up being vaginal. "I felt out of control, and I was embarrassed because I cried out during contractions. I would gladly have had a cesarean, but the operating room was so busy that day they couldn't fit me in. Instead they yelled at me to be quiet."

As stories of fear and a sense of failure came out, the women became eager to tell about their own labors. The nurses gathered around one woman to hug and comfort her when she cried.

One nurse told about a lovely birth experience. Her friend, who was also a labor and delivery nurse, was on duty that day. Her friend sat with her as much as she could while still caring for her other patients, and then she stayed with her after her shift ended and was even allowed to go into the delivery room for the birth.

Layla didn't have to point out the message in that story.

She asked the women if they remembered

something kind and supportive someone did or said while they were in labor. The answers came swiftly. "A nurse wiped a cold cloth across my brow." "The doctor said I was strong." "Someone rubbed my back."

She asked if they remembered something unkind that was said or done, and the answers came even more swiftly. "They got mad at me because they didn't want me to push until they got me to the delivery room, but I couldn't help it." "A nurse told me to shut up; I was bothering the other patients." "They were rough when they moved me onto the delivery table." "The doctor said I wasn't trying hard enough."

"Women remember their birth experiences," Layla told the class. "They need to talk about them. When you get home, ask your mothers and aunts and sisters to tell the stories of their labors."

****

Majid went to the classroom about fifteen minutes after the class was supposed to have ended, but the door was still closed. He eased it open and took a seat at the back of the room.

Hushed female murmuring filled the room. The women huddled in small groups, some standing, some sitting, some clasping hands. Two women had their arms around a third woman who was crying. Layla was with one of the groups, smiling her midwife smile, all compassion and love, her arm draped over the shoulder of one of the youngest nurses.

What kind of class had this been?

Layla spotted him and came to slump into a folding chair beside him, obviously exhausted yet with exhilaration glowing in the depths of her beautiful eyes. He guessed she could use the sort of love and support she'd been giving the other women.

But he couldn't touch her, not in front of his co-workers. Well, not at all really. That one kiss had been an impulsive gesture of friendship when he learned she was staying. He'd tucked that kiss into his heart to be remembered when she was gone. *To torture him when she was gone*. He'd been carefully holding in his feelings since then.

"Was it a success?" he asked, not sure how to interpret the scene before him.

"Yes." She smiled her angelic smile. "We've established a great basis for the rest of the course, and I've made some friends."

"Can you leave?"

"No, I think I'll just sit here in the back of the room until everyone else has left. I won't be long."

He watched, from an uncomfortable plastic chair in a little waiting area outside the classroom, as the nurses slowly drifted from the room. Layla was the last to leave. "Can I get you dinner?" he asked.

"Yes. That would be lovely. "But maybe at your clinic if you don't mind."

So they ate at his desk again. Layla was quiet; she seemed fragile. He asked if she wanted to tell him about the class.

She did. He listened in awe to the passion in her voice as she told what she'd heard.

"There's a huge need for the work you're trying to do, Majid. I'm proud to be a part of it."

What a stroke of luck it had been that she'd walked into his clinic with her jar of semen just when he was ready to start work on the project.

If only he could survive the stroke of fate that had

let her into his heart.

****

She called Dan when she got to her room that evening. "Maybe we should postpone the reception, just for a month; it will be less stressful if I have a little more time."

"No, Layla. I sent out the invitations already. My friend Brittany helped me pick them out and get them addressed. She said if we waited any longer, everything would be booked, so I reserved a party room in a hotel she recommended. I'm sorry, but I just couldn't wait for you to get around to setting things up."

"Oh, okay," she murmured. "Tell me about the hotel. What did you think of it?"

"Honestly, Layla, do you think I have time to check out hotel party rooms? Brittany said it was big enough and fancy enough. I trust her."

"Oh…okay." What else could she say? "What's the name of the hotel? Maybe I could find a picture of it online."

He gave her the name of the hotel and said a stilted goodbye. She hadn't mentioned that she'd be staying in San Francisco for the birth of Rashid and Olivia's baby. She crawled into bed, her mind in turmoil. How could she have gone so quickly from the high she'd felt after the class with the nurses to this panicky feeling that her life was out of control? She opened the Rumi book, and her eyes fell on the quote:

*Maybe in your loud confusion*
*The world will disappear and the curtain lift.*

She felt drawn to the idea that the world might "disappear." She imagined a peaceful void. No responsibilities, no conflict, no indecision. That void beckoned to her.

But what did Rumi mean about a "curtain lifting"? That image evoked fear for some reason. Was she hiding behind a curtain? Could she dare to let it be lifted?

She was normally such a decisive and competent person. What had happened? Look at her. She was afraid to remind her fiancé about her plan to help her sister-in-law in labor, a plan he'd already agreed to, a cheerleader was organizing her wedding reception, and a Behruzi doctor made her heart thump with joy every time she saw him.

Maybe she shouldn't have come to Behruz. The confusion was unbearable.

Her jaw stiffened in resolve. She just had to keep her life on course until she saw Dan again. Then everything would be okay.

Chapter Fourteen

Majid went to the mosque with his parents Friday morning and to their home for dinner afterward.

His mother took a spoonful of hot soup from a pot on the stove and tasted the stew she was preparing. "Is your American friend gone?"

He closed his eyes and took a breath. He hadn't told his mother about the change of plans. He'd been afraid he couldn't talk about it without revealing his feelings. "No, she hasn't. Her uncle convinced her to stay a little longer."

His mother's eyebrows tilted up in sympathy. "Oh dear. Is that good news or bad?"

He wanted to be a little boy who could throw himself into his mother's arms and be comforted. "It's good news, Mother. She's the best possible person to help with the grant application."

"Oh yes, of course. Well that's nice then. Would you like to invite her to the family dinner again this week?"

"That would be great, Mother. Are you sure it would be okay with Father and Grandfather?"

She smiled her motherly smile. "Don't worry about them. I can manage your father, and he can manage his father."

Majid chuckled. It was rare for his mother to acknowledge the power she so delicately wielded in her relationship with her husband. "I'm not sure she'll want to come—some of the aunties were a bit hard on her last time—but I'll ask."

Zora stirred the soup and smiled. "I think your aunts will be a little more friendly this time."

And they were. Soraya came over to greet them as soon as they arrived at his grandfather's home and kissed both of them on the cheek. "How nice to see you again," she said to Layla. His other aunts were more friendly too. The entire atmosphere of the dinner party was mellow.

"What's this all about?" he asked his mother after they'd eaten. "The aunties are practically fawning over Layla."

Zora smiled with eyes that held secrets. "I can't tell you what happened, but let's just say she did a little favor for a few of them."

What could Layla possibly have done to effect such a change in their attitude?

Before he could find her to ask, his cousin Tavo came to tell Majid about headaches he'd been suffering. After asking a few questions and determining that the cause was probably eyestrain from playing too many video games, Majid suggested that Tavo make an appointment for a checkup in the clinic.

When he finally spotted Layla, she was sitting in the corner of the room with his grandfather and his parents.

Uh-oh. Of all his relatives, his grandfather held the strongest prejudices against American women. Majid had introduced him to Layla when she came to dinner the first time, and they'd greeted him tonight, but she'd never really spoken to him. Now she sat on a dainty stuffed chair in front of his couch, apparently engaged in an intense conversation.

He hurried to rescue her, but by the time he reached the little group, all four were laughing. He looked at the two men he loved and respected more than any other men he'd ever met and saw them through Layla's eyes. Grandfather, with his snowy white moustache and his wild mop of white hair, looked like Einstein as an old man, and Father, with hair just beginning to gray, looked like a younger version of the same.

He sat beside Layla. "Everything okay?" he asked her quietly in English.

She answered in Farsi for all to hear. "Hi, Majid. We've been talking about movie stars. About Julia Roberts in particular. She seems to be your grandfather's favorite. Have you seen any of her movies?"

Majid relaxed. She had charmed them, of course. "I'm not as fond of Miss Roberts as Grandfather, but I do like her, and, yes, I've seen several of her movies. I really liked *While You Were Sleeping*."

Layla and Grandfather shook their heads and shared an eye-rolling look of scorn. Grandfather explained, enunciating clearly as if he were speaking to a child, "Julia Roberts isn't in *While You Were Sleeping*. That's Sandra Bullock."

"Oh yes, of course." Majid tried to look appropriately chagrined as the others laughed at his mistake.

"Sandra Bullock is another fine actress, and *While You Were Sleeping* is a charming movie," Grandfather said, and everyone agreed.

Zora described Majid's doula project and Layla's role in helping him. She made a point of noting that Layla would be returning to the States in a week and a half.

"Ah, you're going back to your own people," his grandfather said. He studied Majid for a moment. "Yes, that is good. I'm sure you miss your family."

"Yes, I do," Layla said cheerfully, ignoring the undercurrent in Grandfather's remarks. "I appreciate your kindness in including me in this lovely gathering of your family."

There wasn't anything she could have said that would please Grandfather more than praising his hospitality.

The pregnant cousins joined the group and soon pulled Majid and Layla away. Jala asked, "Can Layla deliver my baby?"

"I'm sorry—she's not certified to practice medicine in Behruz," Majid said.

She turned to Layla. "But Aunt Zora told us you delivered a baby that one time when Majid was stuck at the hospital."

"True, but that was an emergency."

"Well maybe *I* could arrange to have an emergency."

They all laughed.

"Majid is going to deliver your baby, isn't he?" Layla asked and Jala nodded. "In that case, I'll be able to help. I can give you emotional support and suggest position changes that might make things easier for you and your baby. That is, if it's all right with Majid."

Of course it was all right with him. He would love one more chance to work with her. He nodded.

Jala beamed.

He offered to give Layla a ride back to the center of town, and she accepted. They walked to his car, which was parked in front of his grandfather's house.

Before he started the engine, he said, "There's something I have to ask you."

"What?"

"Will you tell me the truth?"

"Not if it's about my uncle. But about anything else, yes."

He smiled. He breathed in her scent. "What was the favor you did that made my aunts suddenly so friendly?"

She smiled her I've-got-a-secret smile. "That's the other thing I can't tell you. I promised."

"Oh, come on. Just this one small thing. I'll never ask another favor."

The smile broadened. She shook her head. "Somehow I doubt that."

He got the key out of his pocket but didn't put it in the ignition. "Please?"

A nearby streetlight illuminated her smiling face. "No. I can't tell you. But…I'm reminded of something I've been wondering about. Can you answer some questions I have about health care in Behruz?"

"Yes, of course."

"Okay. If a menopausal woman were suffering from vaginal dryness, I would, of course, suggest she try some kind of lubricant, but if what she really needed was estrogen cream, would that be available?"

She was talking about one of his aunts, of course. "Yes, she could get estrogen cream. If she had a prescription."

"What if I wanted to write a prescription myself? What would I have to do to get authority to do that?"

"It's not as hard as it would be in the States. You'd have to show proof of your degrees and certifications to the Medical Registration Board. With their approval, you'd be able to practice medicine here just as you did in the States. You could deliver babies."

"I could deliver Jala's baby?"

"You could if you had the approval, but you wouldn't be able to get it in time for Jala's labor. These things take time."

She had a look of stubborn determination on her face. "Yes, but remember how fast the approval came through for the first phase of the grant application? Miracles do happen."

"Yes, I guess sometimes they do." Especially when Layla was involved.

An orange cat came through the wrought iron bars of the neighbor's gate and jumped onto a garbage can a few feet from Majid's car. It sniffed around the edges of the lid and then sat in a sphinx pose looking at the two humans.

"I could get my mom to fax me copies of my diplomas and certifications."

"Don't get your hopes up, Layla. It really would take a miracle for you to get an application approved before Jala has her baby."

"Still, it's worth a try, isn't it?"

"Yes, of course you can try." The cat jumped down onto the sidewalk and ran toward the streetlight. "But, going back to something you mentioned earlier: I should point out that women in this country, especially older women, *menopausal* women, might be too shy to just walk into a pharmacy and ask for vaginal lubricant."

She tilted her head and gave him a coy smile. "In that case I might offer to buy it for the woman."

"You would do that?"

"I think I would...that is...if the situation were ever to arise. But I might give her a few samples from your examining room to try before I bothered to buy some."

"Oh really? You would steal from me?"

Her big, brown eyes were all contrite and innocent. "Possibly."

"And then if the woman found the product helpful, you would buy a tube for her?"

"Yes."

Layla had bought vaginal lubrication for one of his aunts. He laughed. He slapped the palm of his hand on the top of the steering wheel. He couldn't stop laughing.

How was he going to live without her?

When he could speak, he asked, "Wouldn't that be a little embarrassing for you? Buying vaginal lubrication at a Behruzi pharmacy?"

"Yes, it probably would be. But I'll tell you what would be even more embarrassing than that."

"What would be even more embarrassing than that?"

She rolled her eyes and smiled. "If this hypothetical woman had sisters-in-law who also wanted that product, and if all these hypothetical women asked me to stock up for them to be sure they wouldn't run out after I left Behruz, going to the pharmacy for *that* purchase would be really embarrassing."

She joined him in his laughter.

"I can see that would be a challenge."

With eyes big and eyebrows raised, she nodded a knowing *yes*.

"You would do that?"

"Yes. I think I would. And believe me, if I ever did have to buy a bag full of vaginal lubricant in a Behruzi pharmacy, I'd be *very* grateful for the use of a chador to cover my face."

"Yes, I see why you would be. But may I suggest that if a situation such as that ever does present itself, you might consider wearing a lab coat instead of a chador? You could go as a medical provider and stand tall in that role." He was no longer laughing. "In other words, you could go as *who you are*."

"Oh." Her eyes grew big with realization. "I never would have thought of that."

Her gaze drifted away, pensive and grim. The idea must have struck a chord. He waited, trying mentally to force realization in her heart. *Dare to be your truest self. Dare to feel your deepest feelings. And let those deepest feelings be love. For me.*

She was free in so many ways, but something was holding her back.

She said, "I will definitely keep that in mind. *If the situation ever arises.*"

Of course there would be no *forcing* realization on her. She wanted to keep it light. Okay. "So, you still won't tell me what kind of favor you did for my aunts?"

"No. I'm sorry. I can't."

"Well, whatever it was, thank you. You didn't have to do anything for them, not given the way they treated you."

"I was happy to do it. They're nice people. I didn't take their reservations about me personally."

Majid started the engine but left it idling. "Has your uncle's paranoia relaxed a little now that his wife is pregnant? I'd like to take you to his house. I hate seeing you off in a taxi when I'm perfectly capable of driving you."

Layla shook her head. "My uncle is as paranoid now as he ever was. He wouldn't want me to give you any information that would help you figure out who he is."

"Did you explain that doctors are super conscientious about maintaining patient confidentiality?"

"That wouldn't make any difference to him. I guess he's had problems before with people gossiping about his private business."

"Is he a famous entertainer or something? A public figure?"

She sobered and hesitated before answering. "Maybe something like that. Really, I can't say more. I shouldn't be talking about him."

He shifted gears and pulled the car out onto the street. "All right. I'll take you to the clinic then."

He was aching to touch her. As he drove, he thought about the kiss they shared the last time they were alone together in the clinic. What excuse did he have to invite her in tonight? And even if he did, what excuse would he have to touch her? There was no henna tattoo to be examined now and no missed goodbye kiss to make up for.

He had to touch her. Just her hand. Or maybe her lips. He wasn't greedy enough to ask for more.

He could say there was something he needed from his desk. Or there was something he needed to show her, maybe something to do with the grant.

He parked in front of the clinic, opened the door for her, and took her hand to help her out. He didn't release her hand when they stood on the curb. He held it and felt its softness and ached to pull her into his arms.

"Layla, could you come into the clinic for a minute? There's something I…" He didn't know what to say. He hadn't come up with a plan. "Could you just come in please?"

She studied him, waiting for an explanation. He didn't have one. She said yes.

He released her hand while he unlocked the door but then took it again when they were inside. He stood facing her. "Um…let's sit down." He led her to a settee against the back wall of the waiting room, but they didn't sit. She looked at him expectantly. What could he say? What was he asking?

*May I kiss you?*
*You're so beautiful.*
*Don't leave.*
*I can't live without you.*
*I love you.*
*May I kiss you? Just once? Just this once more? I'm sorry: I know you're engaged. I know you love someone else. I'm sorry. Just this once, please?*

No words came. He brushed his fingers across her cheek and down to feel her soft lips. She made a little mewing sound. Her lips parted slightly. An invitation. He took her head between his hands and held it while he bent toward her and claimed those beautiful, irresistible lips.

*A chaste kiss. Just one.*

She leaned into him and wrapped her arms around his torso. Her breasts were molten softness against his chest. Heaven. He dropped his arms to encircle her shoulders and let nature pull the kiss deeper. Her mouth relaxed open, accepting the caress of his lips and tongue.

"Layla." He gulped air and breathed her name. A prayer and a plea. *Layla.* He kissed her. His hands slid down to cup her hips and pull her toward him. They slid up to her waist and then up further, under her T-shirt. Ah, Layla. He swept his hands over flesh he'd never dared dream of touching. Her hands fluttered across his back and then made their way under his shirt. She moaned and sighed and clung to him.

His fingers inched under her bra to touch the side of her breast. *Paradise.* He could sink into that softness and never come out.

She tensed. He pulled his hand away. He pulled his lips away. He said, "I'm sorry."

Her eyes were sad and glazed with desire. She pressed her fingers to his lips. "Don't apologize. I wanted it too."

They gazed at each other. Hopelessly. She tugged the hem of her blouse into place.

He repeated, "I'm sorry."

"You don't have to say that. I'm the one who should apologize." She covered her face in her hands. "I'm so confused."

His breath caught. She was confused. She turned toward the door.

He started to reach for her, but he stopped himself. "Don't leave, not yet, not like this. Please sit for a minute. I'll keep my hands to myself, I promise."

With her arms wrapped around herself, she sat down. "I know I've been giving you mixed signals, and I'm sorry. I do have feelings for you, but I love Dan. I've always loved him. And I've made promises."

Majid sat on the settee beside her, near but not touching. "Yes, I know. You've been clear about that from the beginning. I had no right."

"It's just that working with you like this and seeing you every day has confused me. It's been so long since I've even seen Dan, I'm starting to forget."

"How long has it been?"

"It was last spring, about five months ago, just before he moved. I meant to visit him in Dallas, but I just never had time. I was busy in my practice, and then I was getting ready to come here."

"How long were you engaged before he left?"

Her eyes clenched shut. "He asked me to marry him a week before he left."

"Just a week? You were only together as an engaged couple for one week?"

"Yes. And that week hardly counts. He was busy getting ready for his move to Dallas."

"How long were you together before that?"

She opened her eyes, glanced warily at him, and then turned away. "You're going to laugh at this. It was less than a month. He lived in Los Angeles after college, so I hadn't seen him for several years, but then he came back to San Francisco last April, and we met again, and I guess he just really *saw* me for the first time."

"Only a month? *Less* than a month?" Was she crazy?

181

But then Majid hadn't known her much longer than that.

She leaned back in the sofa. She closed her eyes and sighed.

"I feel guilty about postponing my return. It was selfish of me. It was just that I wanted to see Mina through the most uncertain part of her pregnancy. I wanted to be the one to write the grant application. And I wasn't ready to say goodbye to you."

"But now you are?"

"Oh Majid, no. But I have to. My real life is waiting for me."

"Are you sure that's your real life?"

The anguish and accusation in her eyes seared through him. "Please don't make this any harder than it already is."

"All right."

Anger coiled in his gut, twining with passion, becoming part of it, but he fought it back. He had no right to feel anger. Or passion either.

Later that night, when passion had faded, anger remained.

She'd begged him *not to make it any harder than it already was*.

He'd agreed. He'd allowed her to walk out of the clinic and get into a taxi. He should have objected. He should have kissed her again. Let it be hard. He wanted it to be as hard for her as it was for him.

Chapter Fifteen

Layla lay in bed trying to come to terms with what had happened.

What had she done? She couldn't rationalize not telling Dan about *those* kisses. Fire shot through her veins as she remembered what it was like to be in Majid's arms, to feel his lips on hers, to surrender and lose herself...

She should have been stronger. What was wrong with her? She'd wait until she saw Dan to tell him, of course. Then she'd be able to say it was over and she'd never see Majid again. The moment would have to be just right.

She couldn't imagine a moment that would be right enough for *that* information, and she couldn't imagine Dan forgiving her.

A call from her mother interrupted the torture of her thoughts. She asked her mother to fax the documents she needed for certification.

"Why do you need them, sweetheart? You're coming home in ten days, aren't you?"

"Yes, but there's a young woman here who really wants me to deliver her baby."

Mary laughed. "You seem to have gotten awfully involved in the medical needs of Behruzi women."

"You're right. But, as you predicted, life here would have been a bit boring if I *hadn't* gotten involved."

"I'm not surprised you found something meaningful to do while you're there. It's just what I'd expect from you. But is that the only reason you decided to stay longer?"

"Yes, Mom." Well, it was the *main* reason. Really.

"I'm sure Dan is anxious to have you back. You're not leaving much time for planning the reception in Dallas."

With her free hand, she pulled back the covers. She slid into the luxurious softness of the bed. "Don't worry, Mom. I'll get everything done."

"I know you will, dear. As long as you're sure Dan is the right man for you."

"What do you mean? *As long as I'm sure.* Of course I'm sure."

"Okay, good. That's fine then."

"So you'll fax my documents to the number I gave you?"

"Yes. Is that for a fax machine at the palace?"

"No, Mom, it's the fax machine at Majid's office."

"Oh. Yes of course. Majid is that doctor you mentioned a few times?"

"Yes, Majid is the doctor I've been working with, the one who's trying to get a grant."

"Right. He sounds like a nice man."

Her mother was fishing. She must have heard, or thought she heard, some hint that there were feelings between Layla and Majid.

"Yes, mom. He's very nice. Now I have to go."

She fell into a fitful sleep but woke after about an hour and lay awake with worries and fears and memories of passion swirling in her brain. She lit the lamp on the table beside her bed and picked up the Rumi book, skimming through it until her eyes fell on the passage:

*You must ask for what you really want*
*Don't go back to sleep*
*The door is round and open*
*Don't go back to sleep*

She wanted to throw the book across the room. First her mother inserts a question mark into her plans, and now Rumi tells her to keep seeking.

She came to this country for answers, not riddles and questions.

Screw Rumi. She put the book down and went back to sleep.

\*\*\*\*

Majid sat reading the national newspaper while he ate breakfast. A new project that would bring running water to villages in southern Behruz was being inaugurated. Great. The Behruzi soccer team lost a match to Iran. Darn. And the sultan's wife was expecting a baby. The baby was due in early July.

Early July. That was when Layla's aunt would be having her baby. It was an interesting coincidence, especially considering the fact that her uncle was married on the same day as the sultan. But that was a different uncle from the one whose wife just got pregnant. Or was it? Layla had been vague about that.

Was it a coincidence? Could the sultan be Layla's uncle?

That would explain the need for secrecy when he was seeking help with fertility.

It could also explain the miraculously quick approval of every project that involved her. Approval of her application to provide medical services came through just two days after she filed for it.

But she'd said her uncle never fathered a child, and everyone knew Abu-Khan's American wife did have a baby, the little boy who was killed during the uprising a few years ago.

And another thing: the sultan had been an only child. That meant there was no way he could have a *niece*.

Maybe it was all just coincidence after all.

Majid went early to the clinic to use the computer before Layla got there. A quick online search revealed that Abu-Khan's father had indeed produced only one child. But then a search using the name of the Old Sultan's wife revealed that *she'd* had a son by a first husband before she married Abu-Khan's father.

Bingo. The name of the first husband, who was long deceased, was Mirza Shirvani. Layla's last name was Shirvani. The son of Mirza Shirvani married an American woman and fathered four children, one son and three daughters. He died twenty-one years ago.

Layla would have been seven years old twenty-one years ago.

That was her age when *her father died and her mother took her to live in the States*.

Was Layla one of those three daughters?

He kept searching but couldn't find the name of Mirza Shirvani's son or the names of the son's children, but really the last name and all the other coincidences were enough.

He asked her once if her uncle was an entertainer or a public figure, and she said *maybe something like that*.

Layla must be the sultan's niece.

Wow. That changed everything.

Or did it? She was still an American. She was still smart and funny and irreverent and beautiful. And engaged. She was still leaving soon to go back to America.

And he was still in love with her.

\*\*\*\*

Layla's top pricrity when she woke was calling Dan. She had to tell him about the time she was going to spend in San Francisco for Olivia's labor. She'd call him before going to the clinic. She had to get it over with.

But her cell phone rang before she could place the call. It was Jala's husband, Gaspar. Jala was in labor; they were on their way to the clinic.

She threw on a T-shirt that said *Childbirth: a labor of love*, and hurried to join them.

She worked hard all day, supporting Jala and giving Gaspar ideas on how he could help. Majid came into the room now and then to see how things were going, and he stayed at the end once Jala was in transition. He helped Layla prepare for the birth but stood in the background when it came time to deliver the baby.

Three days had passed since those shattering kisses in the waiting room. Neither of them had mentioned the incident. Majid had been more distant at first, but now they were back to their old rapport. They shared an exultant smile when Jala was finally holding her little baby boy. Gaspar collapsed into Majid's arms.

Layla hugged Jala and clasped Gaspar's hand. She'd decided that rules about touching men didn't apply during the first few minutes after a man has just seen his wife give birth. Majid was standing behind her. Surely the rules didn't apply to a man you've already kissed. Not after you and the man have just shared the challenge and work of bringing a baby into the world. She hugged him too; it was a hug of relief and joy, but it was also a hug of a man and a woman. Her body responded as it had before.

And her heart did too.

It was inappropriate, of course, but no one noticed. All attention was on the baby. Majid whispered into her ear, "I have something to tell you."

"What?"

"Later," he said. "I'll be in my office."

When Layla finished her part of the cleanup she left to join Majid at his desk.

She sat in her usual place across from him. Dinner was already spread out on the desk. She took a bite of the rice.

"I know all your secrets," he said.

What? Was he going to claim to know how she felt about him when she didn't even know herself? All she knew was that she wanted to be with him every minute she could for what remained of her stay. She was afraid of what the answer might be, but she asked, "What secret of mine have you uncovered?"

Indulgence softened his face. "I know that your uncle is our Sultan Abu-Khan Ben Mohamadi."

He knew. Good. She was glad. "How did you figure it out?"

He told her about the announcement of the sultana's pregnancy and all the other clues that fell into place after he realized the sultana was due at the same time as the mysterious aunt.

"So Abu-Khan couldn't wait any longer to announce it." She smiled at Majid. "I'm not surprised you figured it out. Are you going to start treating me with a little more respect now that you know I'm connected to royalty?"

He smiled back. "No."

She shrugged. "Oh. Okay."

"I already had an enormous amount of respect for you. Finding out you have an exalted relative doesn't change anything."

Warmth flushed through her at his compliment.

He tore a piece from the flatbread on his plate. "Does everyone know but me? Is this why all those approvals came through so quickly?"

"No, no one else knows. I'm not exactly sure how it worked, but I imagine someone in the hospital's administration was made to understand it was in their best interest to approve those projects. My relationship with Abu-Khan wouldn't have been mentioned."

"So it wasn't a miracle at all; it was just good old fashioned nepotism—for once working in favor of a just cause."

"I wish I'd thought to appeal to him in the beginning. It might have saved a good deal of work."

"No, it wouldn't have. Everything you wrote for the Health Department approval will be used in the grant application and in implementing the project." He took a sip of tea. "I have one more question: you said your uncle never fathered a child, but our sultan did have a son by his American wife, Karen…"

Oh yes, that. She speared a piece of lamb with her plastic fork. "Since you figured out one secret, I'm going to trust you with another—if you assure me the rules of patient confidentiality still apply."

"Absolutely."

If you repeat what I'm about to tell you to a single living soul, we both risk having our heads hung from the palace gate. Are you sure you want to know?"

He chuckled. "I'm a doctor. I can keep a secret."

"Okay. The baby wasn't really Abu-Khan's."

His eyes widened as that sank in. "You mean his wife had a baby that wasn't his?"

"No. The baby was adopted. That's all I can say. It's really complicated."

"That's amazing. Was the baby really killed in the rebellion?"

"No. The baby's parents are now happily married and raising their son. As I said, it's complicated."

"It's a juicy story. Sharing it might be worth being beheaded."

"The problem with that idea is that I'd be beheaded too."

"Oh yes, I can see how that might be a problem for you. All right then, I'll keep it to myself."

When they were done eating, Majid drove her to the palace and stopped in front of the guard station. Two soldiers approached the car, rifles raised, but when Layla opened the window to show her face they nodded and went back to the station.

She leaned back against the passenger-side door; Majid sat with his arms resting on the steering wheel, turned toward her. They gazed at each other. After working together all day and sharing the satisfaction of welcoming Jala's baby into the world, she felt more bonded to him than ever. Her body clamored for more of the bliss they'd tasted three nights ago, but she couldn't acknowledge that bond and that clamor. She had to break the connection and walk away.

"Goodnight," she said.

"Goodnight, Layla," he replied.

She opened her own door and walked to the guard station.

When she got to her room, she wrote a text to Dan explaining about the time she'd be spending in San Francisco before she came to Dallas.

She didn't have the heart—or the nerve—to tell him directly. *Please, please, please let him understand,* she prayed as she pressed Send.

She opened the Rumi book and read:

> *Let yourself be silently drawn*
> *by the stronger pull of what you really love.*
> *It will not lead you astray.*

There were two strong *pulls* in her case. Two forces that threatened to pull her apart.

Chapter Sixteen

A few nights later, after Majid ate dinner with his parents, his father asked, "When is your American friend leaving?"

Majid tried not to betray how desolate he felt when he answered, "In a week."

"Your mother tells me you've developed quite a regard for the young woman."

"Her name is Layla, Father. And yes, she's been a great help to me. She's an amazing person."

"Have you let her know how you feel?"

What? Did Father know what he was asking? Had he guessed Majid's feelings? Or had his mother told him her conjectures? Was this going to be another guard-your-heart warning about the duplicity of American women?

"I don't know what feelings you're talking about, Father. My relationship with her has been professional."

"I see. I just wanted to be sure you wouldn't be constrained by your uncle's experience and your cousin's—just in case there *were* something you needed to tell her."

"Really Father, I can scarcely believe I'm hearing you say this. I thought you, of all people, would be cautioning me to *hold back* any feelings I might have."

His father smiled and shook his head. "I haven't

changed my impression of American women *in general*, but this particular one does appear to be more mature than the two unfortunates who blundered into our family before. Those two were both young. They interrupted their schooling to get married; they'd never had a real job; and they didn't have any interests that involved them in life here. They didn't even try to learn our language. As a result of all that, they were isolated and lonely."

Majid never thought about how little prepared Amanda and Heather had been to adapt to life in Behruz. He'd had a terrible crush on Amanda when he was fifteen and had been almost as devastated by her defection as his cousin.

"But Layla is engaged, Father."

"I understand that. I'm not suggesting you do anything inappropriate. I just think that if there *is* anything she might need to know about your, uh, *regard* for her, you should tell her. It's not like you to surrender easily to competition."

Wow. The last thing Majid had expected was his father's blessing on his *regard* for an American woman.

\*\*\*\*

Layla gazed at the city spread out below them. She was with Majid in the restaurant at Hotel Abshar, the place where he told her about his family's attitude toward American women. They'd finished eating dinner and were drinking tea. Majid's beautiful, dark eyes gazed at her with such sadness she thought her heart would break. It was time to say goodbye.

It was her last night in Behruz. The grant application had been sent off to the American foundation the day before. They speculated together about how long it would take to hear back.

Majid told her he'd seen Jala's baby, and the little boy was thriving.

They calculated together and decided she would need to leave for the airport at eight in the morning. This time she'd agreed to let Majid take her.

They ran out of impersonal things to say.

The personal things she might have said stung her throat, but she held them back. It had to be a clean break. It would just make things harder if she started talking about doubts. If she spoke of love.

Since there was no longer any need to hide the fact that she was living in the palace, she expected him to drive her there after dinner. But instead of turning north on Karush Street, toward the palace, he turned south.

She didn't ask why. She knew why, and she knew where he was going. But she closed her eyes to the knowledge. She leaned back in the seat and let her mind be blank. No thought, no conversation, no plans, no intention to make love. No.

She sucked in a deep breath, her heart pounding a slow rhythm of excitement and turmoil. She wanted Majid. Every cell of her body yearned for him, but giving in to that yearning would jeopardize everything she'd thought mattered to her.

They arrived at the clinic. He helped her from the car. She waited, hands clenched, while he unlocked the clinic door. She shuffled behind him when he walked to the back of the waiting room.

And then she reached for him. Her heart and her heated body simply overruled her mind and took over. She put her hands on his shoulders and turned her face up to his. His eyes asked *what now?* Without thought of

194

what it meant, she went up on her toes and touched her lips to his. He froze, like an animal gone still when it senses danger. He didn't deepen or even return the kiss, so she rested back down and gazed up at him, waiting. His beautiful dark eyes were so intent, so deep and sad and yearning, that she wanted to open her heart and her body and everything she was to him. But she waited. She watched him watch her, questions in those eyes. And hope.

Then the dam suddenly broke. He pulled her to him and kissed her greedily. Yes. She wanted him out of control. His hunger ignited a deep hungry response in her blood, in her womb. She pressed her breasts against him, and her heart, and the part of her body that was hot and demanding *more*.

Yes.

He drew back for a moment and they gazed at each other, his beautiful dark eyes probing hers, asking, demanding, and…full of love. He closed his eyes and leaned his forehead against hers while they both took deep gulps of air. Still connected, heart, body, and heat.

"Layla, Layla, Layla. Don't leave me."

He kissed her behind the ear, then down the side of her neck and along the ridge of her collarbone: soft, tantalizing kisses that made her forget what was waiting for her on the other side of the world. He slid the neckline of her blouse down out of the way and pressed his lips against the swell of her breast. She melted; she couldn't think; she didn't want to think. Her hand went under his shirt to slide across the taut, muscled flesh of his back.

The shades on the windows of the waiting room were pulled down, but still she felt exposed. He must have felt the same. "Come to my office," he said, and he led her to the room where they'd shared so many meals, so much laughter, and so much unexpressed passion.

They stood in the office and kissed again. His hands were under her shirt; hers were under his. Their movements were slow; her mind was sluggish. She felt drugged.

His desk nearly filled the room. There was no place to be comfortable. He said, "The examining room," and he led her there. He yanked the thin pad from the examining table and dropped it onto the floor. He found blankets and pillows in the linen closet and spread them on the pad. He pulled her back into his arms.

"I'm sorry," he said. "This isn't quite the silken drapes and cushioned couches of your fantasy about love in an exotic land."

She laughed. With her arms around his torso, she pressed her cheek against his chest and felt the rumble of his answering laugh. "It doesn't matter," she whispered.

They sank onto the makeshift bed and kissed again. They lay with arms around each other, bodies pressed together, hearts beating together, until he asked, "Will someone be wondering where you are?"

"Just the guards. They're the only ones who keep track of my comings and goings. I can survive a little disapproval from them."

"It may be very, very late."

"It's okay. Just so I get there in time for my flight."

It was the wrong thing to say. Pain flashed across his face. She slid her palm down his cheek, from his temple to his jaw, feeling the stubble there and the tension. "I'm sorry." She'd said it didn't matter, but now she looked around the room with all its medical equipment and she knew it did matter. And her promise to Dan mattered.

"How can you kiss me like that if you're leaving tomorrow to marry another man?"

Shame merged with the passion pumping through her veins. Her heart thumped hard with lust and *fear*. What was she doing? She could be destroying her future. "I don't know. I can't be sure of anything until I see Dan again. I'm disoriented. It's like I've been in a fairy tale—staying in a palace and working with you. When I get back to my family and my real life, I'll be okay."

She got up onto her knees. She tugged her shirt into place and smoothed it.

Majid got up too and sat cross-legged facing her. "Is *okay* enough for you?"

"I mean my old life will make sense again. People can't live in a fairy tale forever, you know."

"So you think of your time in Behruz as a vacation from your *real life*. Am I the prince in your little fairytale? Have I just been a distraction that makes the fairytale more fun?"

"No, no, no. You're confusing me. You haven't been just a distraction."

"What have I been then?"

She covered her face with her hands. "Don't push me." She stood up. "I'm sorry, I can't do this. It would be wrong. Oh Majid, I am so very, very sorry."

He got to his feet too. He picked up one of the blankets, handed her one end, and began to fold it. They each drew two corners together and doubled it again.

and she handed her half to him to make the final folds. He worked at the job with a doctor's meticulous care. When he was done, he stood with the folded blanket in his arms. "It will have to be washed." His voice was quiet and dead. Moving like a robot—or like a man compulsively erasing the evidence of his folly—he placed the blanket on the examining table and picked up another one. He folded the second blanket, returned the linens to the supply closet, and put the pad back on the table. "I'll get everything cleaned up tomorrow," he said, still in that dead voice. "Let's go."

She followed him to the waiting room. "Maybe I should let one of Abu-Khan's drivers take me to the airport tomorrow."

He stood near the door with his hands in his pockets. "All right, if that's what you want."

"It is. It will be easier."

He reached for the door but didn't open it. He put his hand back in his pocket and faced her, stony pale and bleak. "By all means, let's keep this *easy*. At least for *you*."

She gasped. His sarcasm burned like acid.

He said, "You know I don't want you to go."

*Don't say it. Please*. "Yes, I know that."

"And you know I love you?"

Her heart lurched toward him; her mind recoiled. "Yes, I know that too." She *did* know. Why did he have to say it?

"Okay then, you know I love you and I want you to stay." His eyes were lasers burning that information into her heart. "You've gotten to know my country and my crazy relatives. What remains now for you to figure out is who you are and what you want. What's holding you back, Layla? It feels like you're afraid to live too big a life. Do you want to live as the smart, competent, funny, beautiful person you are? Or do you want to live as the reflection of someone else?"

*Someone else.* Dan. Belonging to him had given her such a sense of security and belonging. What would she have if she didn't have that?

Majid was waiting for an answer. Did marrying Dan mean living as a reflection of him?

No.

Maybe.

No.

Oh crap. She thought again of how impossible it was going to be to explain to Dan what had happened to her in Behruz. What had happened with Majid.

"I need to get back to the palace," she said. The pressure of facing Majid's questions and challenges was too much. She wanted to be *home*. Not in the palace, not in Dallas, not in her apartment, but *home*, in her mother's house, in her old room with her sisters and Rashid and the smell of her mother's cooking. "I want to go."

"All right."

He must have seen the pain on her face and taken pity on her in spite of his anger, for he pulled her into his arms and stroked her back and smoothed her hair as if he were comforting a child. She didn't deserve this comfort; it had been stupid and irresponsible of her to let such strong feelings grow between them. But she would take it. She would soak it up and remember it forever.

Their embrace was quiet like the calm after a storm. He held her for a long time, sliding his hands over her hair, her shoulders, and her back, shushing her as someone might shush a crying baby. Then finally he pulled away and, without saying a word, opened the door of the clinic and led her to his car. They drove to the palace in silence.

Layla watched the now familiar streets and buildings pass out of sight. It was ten o'clock. Shops and businesses were closed and dark, and sidewalks were empty. Would she ever come back? How could she? It would hurt too much to see Majid again.

How could she not? This land was in her blood. And Majid was in her heart.

He stopped the car near the guard station, and Layla lowered her window to let the guards see her face. Majid expelled a defeated sigh. "Will you come back to teach the first batch of doulas if we get the grant?"

She'd dreamed of doing just that, but she had to tell him no. "I'll be busy starting a new job and getting settled."

Majid sat inches away but it might as well have been miles. He asked, "Will you come back to deliver the sultana's baby?"

"I want to." How would Dan take it if she told him she wanted to leave again in pursuit of passions he didn't understand? She remembered him referring to Behruz as "that godforsaken country." She wouldn't be asking—she'd be begging—and the thought of doing it filled her with dread. Still, it would mean so much—to her, to Mina, and to Abu-Khan. And she would see Majid again. "Maybe. I told her I might."

"Well, let me know."

"I will."

How could she say goodbye?

How could she tear herself away?

Tears spilled from her eyes. She said, "I'm sorry."

His eyes blazed frustration and pain. He took her hand, and they sat for several minutes, not speaking, staring ahead at the deserted street. Promises and *maybes* formed in her mind. *I want to come back. Maybe I will come back. I'm not sure how I'll feel when I see Dan.* She didn't speak those *maybes*. It would be unfair to let them torment him as they were tormenting her. She pulled her hand from his grasp, gazed into his beloved face one more time, and then opened the door and slid out of the car. She looked back once as she crossed the street, but the light from the guard station reflected in the window, blocking her view of Majid. The guards said "Salaam, khanoum," and she returned the greeting. She stepped into the guard station where Majid could no longer see her, and waited, tears streaming down her face, wondering in a panic if she was doing the right thing. *Should she have said more? It wasn't too late, was it? She could run back out to him, but what would she say?* She heard when he turned the ignition. Soon the purr of the engine began to move down the street. *Wait.* It grew fainter and fainter and finally faded away altogether.

It was too late.

****

Back in his apartment, Majid read from Rumi:

*The minute I heard my first love story*
*I started looking for you, not knowing*
*how blind that was.*
*Lovers don't finally meet somewhere.*
*They're in each other all along.*

He'd found her, the woman who would be *in him*, in his heart and blood, forever.

And now she was gone.

Chapter Seventeen

"I can't tell you how much I appreciate your being there for me yesterday," Olivia said. Layla was sitting beside Olivia's bed in the hospital. Olivia was sitting up, nursing little Anisa. "I know how anxious you must be to get to Dallas."

"Um...yeah."

"What?"

"What do you mean, *what*?"

"What aren't you telling me, Layla?"

"Dan's kind of unhappy with me for delaying my return. It's been really inconvenient for him to have to take care of everything without me. Our conversations since I reminded him about Anisa's birth have been pretty stilted and uncomfortable."

"Oh, Layla. You should have said something. You should have gone straight to Dallas. I feel terrible."

"No, no, no. Don't feel bad. I wanted to deliver your baby more than anything. I purposely didn't mention Dan because I didn't want to worry you, and I'm sorry I told you now. It's just that he doesn't understand why the trip to Behruz was important to me and why delivering your baby was too. I haven't been able to explain properly, but it will be easier when I see him."

Would it be easier? She imagined it being like an inquisition. Her reunion with Dan should be joyful—

hopefully it would be—but the explanations and apologies she would have to produce could sour everything.

Anisa made a slurpy sound and fell off the breast, asleep. Olivia adjusted her gown and settled the baby in her lap. "Oh Layla, you have to go now. Go today."

"I have a reservation for a flight tomorrow. "

"Good. Does he know you're coming?"

"Yes. I just sent him a text with my flight details."

"Don't worry. He loves you. Everything will be fine."

"I hope so."

Olivia lifted her gaze from the baby to Layla, speculation in her eyes. "Is there something else you're not telling me?"

"No."

"Are you sure?"

"Actually, I've been a little confused." What an understatement that was. "I met someone in Behruz."

Olivia studied Layla. "It's the doctor, isn't it?"

"Yes. How did you know? I haven't told a soul."

"Oh, my dear. He comes up in your conversation rather a lot, and every time he does you go all moony."

"Yes it's Majid, but nothing happened. That is, not much happened. Well, okay, a lot happened, but we didn't do...well, you know... Anyway, I'll never see him again, so it's over, but it has confused me. I think I'll be fine when I get to Dallas. I've just gone too long without seeing Dan."

"All right. Just so you don't feel you have to go through with the engagement. You can change your mind if it doesn't feel right."

"I'm sure it's right, Olivia. Dan and I are like you

and Rashid. You two were friends ever since you were teenagers. You had a crush on him all that time, and look how happy you are now. It will be the same for me and Dan."

"Oh, Layla," Olivia replied, "no relationship is just like any other. I hesitate to be the one to point this out, but you hardly knew Dan at all before last spring, and you didn't really spend much time with him then. When Rashid and I finally acknowledged our love, we already knew each other; we'd been true friends through our teen years. Our long history enriches our relationship, but it's not what makes it work. Love is. Adult love. Common interests and goals are. Jamal and Anisa are." She took a deep breath and said solemnly, "Don't place too much importance on the crush you had when you were a child."

That wasn't what she was doing. She'd been so happy during the time she spent with Dan last spring. When she saw him again, she'd get that magic back.

Later, in her old room in her mother's house, memories of Behruz washed over her like waves in the sea. She thought of Zora, so strong and kind, and of the women she'd helped in labor: Nida, Darya, and Jala. Other memories—of Mohammed's delicious food, camels walking down the street, and the crazy, jumbled world of the bazaar—scrambled together in an exotic mosaic in her mind. Abu-Khan had been exasperating sometimes, but all she could remember of him now was his sweet dedication to Mina. She thought wistfully of the joy that awaited them when their baby was born.

And she remembered Majid. His kind doctor's smile, his Nike tennis shoes, his intense, dark eyes. His lips on her lips. His hands on her body. Majid. His name was a song in her heart. A sweet, sad song. Would memories of him always be painful?

She hadn't heard from him since she left. Should she call him? No. It would be wrong. Nothing had changed. It would just be painful for both of them.

But…

She reached for her phone.

Just a text. An impersonal one. A tiny thread of connection.

She sent him a brief message about the birth of Olivia's baby.

\*\*\*\*

Majid read again the text he received from Layla the previous day. *Baby Anisa born last night. 8 pounds, 4 ounces. Everyone healthy and happy.*

The baby had been born. That meant Layla was on her way to Dallas. She could be with the blond Adonis now. Jealousy churned in his belly, but hope stirred too. If she had to see the football coach in order to know her own heart, then he was glad the time had come.

He wouldn't call. Even though it took all the self-control he could muster, he would let this one more day pass without calling. Still, he couldn't resist responding to her text. He typed a brief message. Just a few references to Rumi:

*The third on p 45, the last on p. 51, and the fourth on p. 97.*

\*\*\*\*

Layla squirmed in her seat, trying to find a position comfortable enough to allow her to sleep. The long flight from Behruz, the time change, and then Olivia's all-night labor had left her exhausted. Adrenaline had kept her going until now, but it was gone and her system was crashing. If only she could sleep a few hours on the plane, she'd be in better shape to face Dan. It was going to take such *effort* to get back to the easy, loving relationship they had before he went to Dallas. She needed to be at her best. She needed *sleep*.

The businessman sitting next to her cleared his throat and shifted away from her efforts to get comfortable.

"Excuse me," she said.

He didn't reply.

She pulled the Rumi book from her purse to read the quotes referenced in Majid's text. Her vision clouded with tears, blurring the words, but it didn't matter. She knew them by heart. The three quotes ran together in her mind, making a poem of love just for her.

*Don't waste your life with those who do not see you.*
*Come back. Brighten my eye, even if I don't deserve it.*
*You are the sky my spirit circles in,*
*the love inside love ...*

She pictured a graceful bird circling in an open sky. She longed for the stillness of that circling bird. The calm and peace and certainty of Majid's love echoed in her heart like a prayer, but the momentum of her life kept her hurtling onward through stormy clouds toward Dan.

As soon as she passed through airport security, she saw him, standing with the crowd on the other side of the barrier. Dear Dan, the man she'd adored since she was twelve years old. He was dressed all in maroon, with the word *COACH* emblazoned on his chest in gold. Maroon and gold must be the school colors. She should have known that. He was the tallest man in the crowd and the most handsome. He stood with his shoulders squared and his head held high in a confident, man-in-charge stance. A coach's stance.

She threw her arms around him when she reached him, and he held her for a moment. "Well, finally," he said.

"Are you still mad at me?"

He grinned down at her with his usual affection and indulgence. "I thought I was, but now that I see you, I can hardly remember why." He cuffed her teasingly under the chin. "I'm sure you'll make it up to me."

That was it? It was that simple? Relief flooded through her until she remembered the confessions she had yet to make.

He took her carryon bag and set out with his long strides toward the baggage claim.

She wondered what he meant about "making it up to him." He'd probably expect her to defer to him when they had a difference of opinion. He'd drop a hint about her "indebtedness" and she'd go along with whatever it was he wanted. She knew what that felt like. Hadn't she always been "making it up" to him—for being the golden boy who rescued her from the wretchedness of not fitting in? For being her key to a life of acceptance?

A key to acceptance that came from outside herself. *From him.*

Did she still need that? He beamed the happy, possessive smile that had always warmed her in the past. Now it seemed tinged with arrogance. She hadn't noticed that before. She didn't feel warmed.

"We'll go home to get you freshened up," he said when they were waiting for her bags. "We have a dinner with the other coaches tonight. I can't wait for them to meet you."

"Oh Dan." She couldn't hide her disappointment. "I'm exhausted. I was hoping to rest before I had to meet people."

"I'm sorry, Layla, but this has been planned for a long time. I have to be there, and I need you by my side. I'll fix you a cup of coffee when we get home. That will perk you up."

Dan maneuvered the car through whizzing traffic on freeways that were a maze of overpasses, underpasses, and off-ramps. The only sights were dry, vacant fields, jumbo office buildings, and acres of parking lots. Finally he pulled the car into the underground parking lot that lay beneath his twelve-story apartment building.

"Voila," he proclaimed when he opened the door to his apartment on the eighth floor. "Your new home."

The apartment was spacious, with gleaming wood floors and a bright kitchen, but it felt impersonal. All the furniture—the mahogany dining table, glass coffee table, Naugahyde sofa, and the matching chair—were spanking new and flashy. Her mind started to work, imagining how she would make it homier, but Dan wouldn't want her to replace what he'd already bought, and she wouldn't want to criticize his taste, so what could she do? Oh dear, there was a picture next to the dining table of dogs playing poker. Would she be able to replace at least that without hurting his feelings?

A shelf unit in the entryway was filled with pictures and trophies celebrating Dan's glory days as an athlete and his achievements as a coach. Nestled among the pictures of teams he'd played on and teams he'd coached was one of her and him together, taken about six months ago at a party honoring one of the stars of the San Francisco Giants baseball team.

She'd felt beautiful that night. "Buy a new dress," Dan said a week before the party. "Get something feminine and sexy."

Not wanting to spend money for a dress she'd probably only wear once, Layla borrowed one from her older sister Salma. Now she gazed at the picture, remembering how she felt wearing that pink, strapless gown. Padding she'd added to the bosom—because Salma was better endowed than she was—chafed her nipples, and she had to keep her back slightly arched to keep the bodice from falling down, but even so, she felt like a princess. She reveled in Dan's pride as he introduced her to his jock friends. He told her half a dozen times how beautiful she looked.

Ever since she was twelve years old she'd dreamed of hearing him say that. She'd longed for him to notice and *appreciate* her. That night he had. She remembered the joy she felt. She'd been with *Dan*. Her dream had come true.

Had Majid ever told her she was beautiful? She didn't think so, but the admiration in his eyes had screamed it again and again. She thought back. He had said it once, in an indirect way, when he asked, "Do you want to live as the smart, competent, funny, beautiful person you are, or do you want to live as the reflection of someone else?"

Was the Layla in that picture just a reflection of Dan's pride in her? The picture showed the woman her twelve-year-old self had hoped she would become, not the woman she actually was.

If Dan thought he was marrying the woman in that picture, he was going to be disappointed. Little jagged pieces of her real self would keep poking out.

Dan watched her study the picture and gave her an affectionate smile. "You were gorgeous that night, darlin'. I was very proud of you." He touched his fingertips to the photo. "Sit down and relax. I'll fix you a drink."

Back in the living room, she fell into a recliner and leaned back.

She gulped the drink he brought her, choking as it burned her throat. She'd been without alcohol for seven weeks and hadn't missed it. "Didn't you say something about coffee?"

"Oh, yes, right, I did, but, come to think of it, it would be easier to get that on the way to the dinner. How about some water for now?"

"Okay. That would be nice."

He got her a glass of water and sat on the sofa facing her. He spread out his arms along the back of the sofa, king of his domain, and gave her a loving, possessive smile.

She sipped the water, which was lukewarm and tasted of chlorine. She really needed that coffee. Why hadn't she insisted? Was she going to spend a lifetime wearing uncomfortable dresses and pretending her own needs didn't really matter?

She dreaded the dinner to come: the small talk, the glad-handing, and the endless conversations about plays and players.

She realized she couldn't do it.

It seemed impossible to own up to the mistakes she'd made, but this city, this apartment, and *this man* would never feel like home.

*Try going as who you really are*, Majid had said.

Could she expose who she really was? To Dan? After more than a decade of trying to be other than who she was *for* Dan?

Rumi said:

> *Someone who does not run*
> *toward the allure of love*
> *walks a road where nothing lives.*

The truth crashed down on her and left her with no choice. She'd loved Dan with a child's adoration, so blinded by a twelve-year-old's needs that she never got to know him as an adult.

It wasn't his fault she hadn't really known him. He'd always been open about who he was. Majid had been right: the person she hadn't known, at least when it came to love, was herself. Dan was a good man and an honest man, but he wasn't *her* man.

She'd adored him and made promises to him, but now she had to say, *Oops, I'm sorry but I've just realized I don't really know you. I'm afraid I didn't really know myself.* How could she be so fickle? She felt like the shallow, heartless female Majid's family thought all American women were.

But it would be more contemptible still to marry him.

Chapter Eighteen

Layla stood when she heard the announcement, *"Now boarding flight number 7865 for Frankfurt."* She'd gone through the agony of trying to explain everything to Dan, not that he understood even after all her efforts, and she'd flown back to San Francisco. She'd slept three nights in the home of her mother, who fed and pampered her and who *did* understand. She'd held Olivia and Rashid's new baby and played catch with their little boy.

She'd contacted the Behruzi embassy to make sure her visa was still valid and had bought a silk scarf for Majid's mother.

She'd packed everything she'd brought to Behruz the first time plus teaching materials and a few more funny T-shirts. Her mother would ship the things she couldn't take on the plane.

Her mother even promised to return everything in that mountain of shower gifts.

Now she was boarding the flight that would be the first leg of her trip back to Behruz. Back to Majid.

She should sleep—this trip would be exhausting— but her mind was busy rehashing regrets.

It had been stupid of her to mistake a childish infatuation for love and it had been irresponsible to make promises to Dan when she didn't really know him, but she had the feeling he'd recover rather quickly.

She suspected the cheerleading coach she'd been hearing about might be happy to learn the wayward fiancé was out of the picture. And if that woman didn't turn out to be the salve to his bruised ego and heart, then surely there would be others who appreciated his status and who shared his interests more than Layla ever had.

Regrets gave way to the excitement of thinking about all she could do in Behruz. She could work with Majid, delivering babies. She could prescribe hormones for menopausal women and help with all the other aspects of women's reproductive health. She could train the first recruits in the doula project.

She could help Mina give birth to a new prince or princess for Behruz.

She could use her influence with Abu-Khan to humanize childbirth and improve healthcare in Behruz.

She could make love with Majid.

She could marry him and show his doubting family a thing or two about the faithfulness and dedication and spunk of American women. Or at least one American woman.

She would wear a chador sometimes when she didn't want to call attention to her Americanness, but she would go without one when she needed to honor her liberated Western self.

She'd worn a chador one afternoon in San Francisco when she was running errands, just to see what it felt like to proclaim her Behruzi heritage. There were a few curious stares, but she ignored them. She stood tall and proud, feeling giddy in the knowledge that *she knew who she was*. She was both American and Behruzi.

Majid didn't know she was coming. She wanted her return to be a fact when she told him, not a promise. She'd call when she got there.

On the long flight from San Francisco, she thought of Rumi's words:

*You have escaped the cage.*
*Your wings are stretched out.*
*Now fly.*

She *was* flying. She would soon be in Majid's arms.

No one met her at the airport in Behruz City. She hadn't told Abu-Khan she was coming either. She wanted time alone with Majid before Abu-Khan and Mina began making demands on her.

She changed money in the airport and found a taxi out front. She asked the driver to take her to Hotel Abshar.

It took all the discipline she could muster not to call right away, but after the flight to Frankfurt, the three-hour layover there, the flight to Tehran with a layover there, and the final flight to Behruz City, she was exhausted. She had to be rested when she saw Majid.

Fortunately, long nights working as a midwife had taught her how to sleep under any circumstances. When she got to the hotel, she went to bed and slept until morning.

She woke at eight-fifteen. Majid would already be at the clinic. Her fingers shook as she placed the call.

"Layla," he said when he answered. Her name was an endearment and a prayer. "Where are you?"

"I'm here. Hotel Abshar. Room 9."

He was silent for a moment. Had he heard? Did she

need to explain?

His voice was gruff when he answered. "I'm on my way."

He was on his way. Poor Saba would have to deal with the disappointed patients in the clinic. That didn't matter. Nothing mattered. Majid was on his way. She took a shower, brushed her teeth, and went back to bed, her whole body tingling with anticipation.

He was coming. She got up again and applied a slight mist of scent. She brushed her hair. She rifled through her suitcase until she found a T-shirt he'd never seen. She took off her nightgown, put the T-shirt on over a pair of bikini panties, and went back to bed.

At last there was a knock at the door.

He stood motionless for a moment, gazing at her, at her bare legs, at her face, which must surely show all the love she felt, and at her T-shirt. Color slashed across his cheeks when he read the words written on the front of that shirt, *Support your local midwife. Make love.*

He lifted her into his arms and kissed her. Then he carried her into the room and closed the door. "I've missed you. I love you. When did you come? Why didn't you tell me you were coming? What happened? Tell me everything." It all came out in a rush; he didn't wait for answers; he kissed her again before she could speak.

"I love you," she said when he broke the kiss for an instant.

Love and hope and longing gleamed in his moist eyes. "How long are you staying?"

"Forever."

"Forever," he repeated.

"I'll want to visit my family now and then, but

Behruz will be my home. *You* will be my home."

"How I've dreamed of hearing you say that." His hands swept up and down her back. He covered her face with eager kisses.

He led her to the bed, and they stretched out on their sides facing each other, drinking in the sight of each other. He took her hand and held it against his chest. She felt the frantic beating of his heart. She told him about the birth of Olivia's baby and about Dallas and what she realized when she saw Dan.

He laced his fingers through her hair, raking it back away from her face, and then slid his hand down to trace her eyebrows, her cheeks, and her jaw. His fingers shook against her skin.

"I can't believe you're really here. I can't believe I finally have the right to touch you." His expression was so tender it would have melted her heart if her heart weren't already a puddle of soppy love. "Just a few hours ago, I awoke to start another day of a life without you, and now you're here."

The fingers of his free hand drifted across her T-shirt, tracing the letters. He read the words as he touched them. The first line, *Support your local midwife*, led his fingers across the top of her breasts, teasing, tickling, tantalizing.

When he got to the second line, *Make love*, his hand slowed even more. He spelled out the words one letter at a time, inching his fingers across the fullness of her breasts, loving and tormenting each nipple in its turn.

He said, "I got here as fast as I could. I didn't think to bring, uh, you know…."

She laughed. "Condoms? I thought of that." She

rose to produce a box from the table beside the bed and to slip off her T-shirt and panties. He stood to remove his clothes too and then lay facing her again.

Her body clamored for his touch but at the same time reveled in this state of hungry, humming anticipation. She remembered the picture of a seagull in Majid's office. She felt like that seagull, hovering over the waves, sighting a morsel that would relieve its hunger, ravenous and ready to swoop but waiting, filled with the stillness of destiny.

Majid's nostrils flared. His rasping breath was the only sound in the room. She watched him look at her, saw the desire and love in those lush, intense eyes. He gazed at her blatantly, at her nipples, which swelled as if he were touching them again, at her belly, at her hair stretched out across the pillow. No one had ever looked at her like this. No one had ever *seen* her like this. She'd let him see her heart and soul. Now she was letting him see her body. She was at rest being seen and loved by him—with nothing to fear, nothing to prove. She felt timid and brazen at the same time.

Majid's lips spread in a tender caress of a smile. Moisture pooled in the corners of his eyes. "You brought protection. So you were planning on seducing me?"

"Actually, since I'm not quite recovered from the trip, I was hoping you would seduce me. If getting you in the mood is going to require a lot of effort on my part, maybe it should wait a day or two."

"Oh my darling Layla, my beloved 'local midwife,' it cannot wait another day, not another minute." They reached for each other in the same moment and rolled into each other and wrapped arms and legs around each other and, finally, let their bodies find home in each other. She gasped. She cried out. She clung to him as waves of piercing pleasure swept through her. He cried out too, an exultant cry into her hair, and collapsed with his arms still around her, his heart pounding against her breast.

She'd barely recovered—her breathing hadn't returned to normal—when she felt the heat was still there and was building once again. It was the same for him; she felt his desire grow. She smiled at him shyly, so exposed and open, so in love. "Wow."

"Wow indeed."

They made love again, more slowly and reverently, with time for words of love and moans and sighs. With time to build to an even more exquisite end. Afterward, she lay with her head on his shoulder in that place she once yearned to claim as her own and felt the pure joy of possibility. She was free to explore this man—his body, his heart, his amazing mind, his life. And to explore her own potential. A new life, *with Majid*. A new home, *with Majid*. New work. A city to explore. A country to explore. *With Majid*.

Her own body and heart and mind to explore— with this new awareness that *she was enough.*

He smoothed damp hair away from her perspiring face and kissed the top of her head. "You have a gray hair here. Did you know that?"

"No, I do not have a gray hair."

"Yes, you do. I can prove it. Do you want me to pluck it?"

"No! Let it be. It's a symbol of the old age we're going to spend together."

He gazed into her eyes as if they held the universe.

219

"Say it again."

She smiled. "We're going to grow old together, Majid."

"That's an amazing prospect, but it's not what I meant."

"What then? That I love you?" She didn't wait for his answer. "Majid, I love you."

"No, not that. Well, yes of course that—I'll never tire of hearing you say that—but tell me again how long you're staying."

She held his head between her flattened hands and kissed the corners of his eyes. She kissed the bridge of his nose, his cheeks, his chin. "Forever."

"Every day after you told me you weren't really married, when you told me you were leaving in three weeks, I counted how many days I had left with you. Now I can start counting the days of our life together."

"Well, Day One has been memorable."

He laughed. "Beloved Layla, Day One has been the most memorable day of my life. It's the day you came back to me with a heart open to love."

She grinned. "I'm hungry. I haven't had breakfast."

They dressed and went to the restaurant, where she ate an enormous breakfast. Then they strolled in the gardens and followed a trail to the waterfall. They stopped when they reached the pool at its base and stood surrounded by dahlia bushes with their bright display of flowers that would soon be killed by autumn frosts. To their right, the cascade of water glistened in the midday sun. Beside it, on either side, willows splashed long graceful branches into the pool. To their left, almost halfway around the pool from them, a gardener was pruning rose bushes, cutting them back to bare stubs and throwing the prunings into a cart.

Majid took her hand. "I never gave up hope that you'd come back to me."

"I think in my heart I always knew I would."

"My aunts and uncles are going to go crazy when they find out you're related to their beloved sultan."

"Don't tell them right away. I want them to accept me for who I am."

"I believe you've already won them—with your charm and wit and beauty and grace and with your knowledge of pregnancy, your willingness to buy female products, and your enthusiasm for Julia Roberts—but I'll wait to tell them if you want me to. They will find out when your illustrious relatives show up at our wedding."

"Right. Well you can tell them before then." She sighed. "I was imagining a wedding in the States, something simple—I don't have the energy to plan another bash like I was supposed to have with Dan— but right now the idea of flying halfway around the world seems exhausting. Could we get married here? I think my family would come."

"Yes, we can get married here. My family will love it."

"Do you think someone else could plan it? I want a henna party, but other than that I don't care about a single detail."

"I don't either. You are the only detail that matters to me."

"Whoever planned Abu-Khan's wedding can coordinate with your mother and your aunts. All I want to know is where to go and when to show up." She snuggled under his arm. "Can we live together before

221

the wedding?"

"I don't think we should. Which brings up the question—how long do you want to wait?"

A soft breeze rustled the leaves of the dahlias and rippled the water of the pool. "I've been thinking about that. What's the usual length for an engagement in this country? I don't want to shock the natives."

"I can't wait. Let's shock the natives. They'll get over it."

His show of defiance made her smile. "I must be a bad influence on you if *you're* the one suddenly willing to ignore convention."

"Yes, my dear Layla, you are a deliciously bad influence on me." He squeezed her hand, which was still nestled in his. "Since today is Day One of our life together, let's say our vows now. Then whatever wedding Abu-Khan and my relatives come up with will be a mere formality."

She raised herself up on her tiptoes and kissed him. "Yes. This is the perfect setting."

The gardener, a miniature old man wearing a turban and baggy clothes of the sort worn in the villages, had paused in his work, his pruner in one hand, a rose branch in the other. He seemed to be watching them. What did he see? An American woman? Or a Behruzi woman? She smiled at him. He tilted his head and went back to his work. Maybe what he saw was just a woman in love.

"Just a minute," she said to Majid. "Wait here." She hurried, nearly dancing, along the path around the pool to where the gardener was working. "Salaam alaikum, esteemed elder," she said.

"Salaam, khanoum." He touched his forehead.

"I was wondering—" She motioned to the prunings in his cart. A few still bore the last roses of the season. "Could I have a couple of those?"

"Why yes, of course, khanoum. He carefully selected three of the most perfect roses. "Will these do?" They were pale pink and lovely.

"Yes, Agha, they are beautiful."

She reached for them, but he said, "Wait a second." He slid a single blade of the pruner along the stem of one of the roses, skillfully slicing off the thorns. He repeated the process with all three stems and handed her the three roses, now smooth and safe to hold.

"Thank you, Agha. You are very kind."

He bowed, looking pleased, and she ran back to the man she loved.

She held the roses like a bridal bouquet as they declared their love and their commitment—using words they'd already spoken and adding new declarations and promises, interrupting each other eagerly and kissing often.

The gardener watched from the other side of the pool, a witness to their exchange of vows.

And a second witness, Rumi, smiled from heaven.

*The world will disappear and the curtain lift.*

## A word about the author...

Judy was born in Kansas and raised in Minnesota. She now lives with her husband Jim in a small town in Oregon, where she works as a doula and childbirth educator. Her free time is devoted to grandmothering, gardening, embroidering, beachcombing, traveling, and, of course, writing.

Thank you for purchasing
this publication of The Wild Rose Press, Inc.

If you enjoyed the story, we would appreciate your
letting others know by leaving a review.

For other wonderful stories,
please visit our on-line bookstore at
www.thewildrosepress.com.

For questions or more information
contact us at
info@thewildrosepress.com.

The Wild Rose Press, Inc.
www.thewildrosepress.com

Stay current with The Wild Rose Press, Inc.

Like us on Facebook

https://www.facebook.com/TheWildRosePress

And Follow us on Twitter
https://twitter.com/WildRosePress